T0086316

How to Rob a
Nice Old Lady

Bill Mooney

HOW TO ROB A NICE OLD LADY

iUniverse books may be ordered through booksellers or by contacting:

iUniverse
1663 Liberty Drive
Bloomington, IN 47403
www.iuniverse.com
844-349-9409

Because of the dynamic nature of the Internet, any web addresses or links contained in this book may have changed since publication and may no longer be valid. The views expressed in this work are solely those of the author and do not necessarily reflect the views of the publisher, and the publisher hereby disclaims any responsibility for them.

Any people depicted in stock imagery provided by Getty Images are models, and such images are being used for illustrative purposes only. Certain stock imagery © Getty Images.

ISBN: 978-1-6632-2336-4 (sc)
ISBN: 978-1-6632-2337-1 (hc)
ISBN: 978-1-6632-2335-7 (e)

Library of Congress Control Number: 2022915506

Print information available on the last page.

iUniverse rev. date: 08/18/2022

She is a a fine researcher and a great friend.
With admiration and affection, this work is
dedicated to

Maxine Stonehill

CHAPTER 1

It Begins

It was just a tick after seven thirty in the morning when he emerged from the Sixty-First Street apartment building and took up a position on the stoop. He inhaled a couple deep breaths and smiled. It was going to be a good day. He moved quickly down the twelve steps to the pavement and looked skyward. The unusually late fall that had seemed to be so reluctant to give way to the onset of winter had disappeared now. It was cold, yet it still gave the city one of those brilliantly sunny, frosty days that New Yorkers are justified in bragging about.

He drew in a couple more breaths of the cold air, and in a few brisk strides, he reached the sidewalk. He stood there for a moment, looking for any sign that a taxi might be coming his way.

He was a good-looking man in his mid-thirties with well-trimmed brown hair and blue eyes. His movements were deliberate and precise. But at the same time, he conveyed an impression of calm and self-confidence, together with a look about him that indicated athleticism. Yet there was no sense of self.

The slim briefcase he carried and his clean-cut appearance confirmed the attention to the trimmings of a city businessman.

He was neatly turned out in a medium-grey suit with a white shirt and blue necktie. He had decided against the tie matching just-for-show top pocket handkerchief that Mr Markham frequently sported. He wore polished black shoes, and over one arm, he carried a lightweight topcoat. He was on his way to set in motion events that would change his life forever.

The janitor was busy attaching something to one of the lower windows.

'Morning. Cabbing it today, eh?'

'Hi, Tim. I was going to, but maybe I'll walk it. There won't be too many days like this from now on.'

'You know it.'

'Oh, well, yeah. It's cold, but it's like, like a champagne day.'

'Champagne, huh?' Tim said, wondering what the hell that meant. 'Kinda early for you today, ain't it, Mr Wheeler?'

'Little bit.' He smiled. 'You know, Tim, it's not really like winter at all.'

'You think so? Well, maybe today ain't so bad, but don't worry,' Tim said, adding a *brrrr* sound. 'It's comin', cold, cold, and very cold. Oh, yeah, it's comin' all right.'

'I suppose.'

'Next week, we'll all be shivering. You can bank on it.'

'Well, it's nice today, and that's what matters.'

'Big day?'

'Oh, yeah,' he said and laughed. 'I'm banking on it!'

Steve Wheeler donned the topcoat and called over his shoulder, 'See you, Tim.'

He strode off towards Fifth Avenue and onward, heading towards mid- and lower Manhattan. A few blocks later, however, he did flag down a cab that took him closer to his destination. He got out, paid the cabbie, and walked the rest of the way.

Steve stood, looking at what appeared to be an abandoned building site. It was—or was planned to be—an office block on the lower south side of Sussex Street, near Delancey, close to what might be the outer limits of Lower Manhattan. It was to be a relatively small building when compared to the massive skyscrapers not much more than a block away. It was planned to be only nine stories high when completed, somewhat similar to other buildings in the vicinity.

Work stopped some months before, and it didn't seem likely construction would restart anytime soon. The reason, as is so often the reason, was that the property developer, due to unforeseen circumstances, had run out of money. They—the developers— were looking for financing or someone to buy the property. Until something of that nature happened, it would stay as it was, dormant, and, to say unfinished would have to be an understatement, with major construction barely started. Since even vandals would have little interest in such a place, it was left unattended, security apparently unnecessary. It was just one of a number of other building sites dotted around several parts of the city that had suffered the same financial woes and were pretty much in the same incomplete state.

The site was surrounded by the usual high, wooden contractor's fence, but there was easy access at the rear. The work had only progressed as far as the basement and a steel and concrete skeleton of two floors above that. Right now, it looked as though the whole thing would have to start over if it were ever going to come to anything. No doubt it would stay as it was for some considerable time. It suited Steve's purpose perfectly.

He went in through the opening of the fence at the back and walked forward across the rough ground until he came to another opening with stairs that took him to the basement. Steve stepped gingerly downwards, placing one foot carefully in front of another to avoid the cement rocks and other building debris scattered on the unfinished stairway.

As he neared the basement floor, he noted that two deep holes had been dug in preparation for the elevator shaft machinery yet to be installed. And several other holes awaited slabs of concrete to be placed over them. There were a number of those concrete slabs heaped unevenly with several others of the same stacked against the wall.

Thin streaks of light crept through the cracks of the floor above, and there was a smell that only a building in that particular unfinished state can produce: wood, cement, and damp earth.

Four men were in the basement quietly watching him as he stepped downwards and all the way until his arrival at the basement floor.

The four men were separated from each other as much as seemed possible in such a small space. One of them, a big man but in no way a fat man, was leaning back easily on a stack of building blocks. In contrast, one or two of the others moved a little, shuffling their feet around on the cold unfinished floor.

Steve moved towards them with the same careful steps as when coming down the stairs. He looked at them, and they looked at him, creating an atmosphere of anticipatory stillness in the already noiseless below-street level chamber. The man who outsized the others stood and moved closer to Steve. The others, as though taking his lead, walked over to form a group of five. Steve took a moment before speaking.

'Good morning,' he said quietly, smiling. 'It's good to see that you are all here as agreed.'

An awkward few moments of silence followed. Steve looked at the four men, varying in age, stature, and character. The big man, around the mid- to late-sixties in age, was about to say something. But it was one of the others, Johnny, who spoke first. 'So, what now?'

'Of course.' Steve nodded. 'The four of you showing up here today constitutes the sealing of the deal. What I have planned cannot be accomplished without each of you and all of you. If any of you didn't appear today, the deal would be off.'

He took a moment as though organizing his thoughts and then continued.

'Right now you are strangers to each other. But that will change very soon. For now, first names will be all right.'

He looked directly at the older man, big and tough with a barrel chest and hefty arms that seemed to be ready to burst through the winter jacket that he wore. 'I'm Matt', he said, smiling genially. 'Okay?'

'Fine, Matt.'

'Good.'

Steve nodded and was about to say something when the youngest of them seemed as though he couldn't get his information out fast enough. 'Luke, and ah', he answered a little nervously. He was in his late twenties, small in stature, and skinny, with a boyish look. 'Yeah, I'm Luke.'

The next man to speak was in his late-thirties and quite tall. He was a well set up, heavily muscled man, obviously made strong from many years of hard work. 'Okay, I'm Johnny,' he said quietly but with an assertive New York pitch of voice.

'And I'm Mark.' This from a neatly dressed man of about the same age as Johnny but quite different in every other way, and not only because he spoke with more than a trace of a cultured accent. He mirrored Johnny, however, in that he also had a fine physique. But unlike the hard worker Johnny, his came from a strictly adhered to gym regimen.

A breeze whistled gently through the unfinished steel and concrete works above them. Only an occasional impatient car horn was heard from the street as Steve took a measured glance at this divergent group before speaking.

'Well, first off', he began, 'it is important for you to know that your personal history has been thoroughly researched by me. And, of course, I have met with each of you separately on more than one occasion before I brought you all together. Mark, you look like you have something to say?'

'Oh, nothing really', Mark said in a clipped, precise manner. 'I suppose what I have to say is that this is the two craziest things I've ever heard of. The first crazy is that this thing could ever be done.'

He's British, Johnny thought. Well, he had nothing against the British that he could think of, except maybe the snooty way some of them talked.

'What's the second?' Luke wanted to know.

'The second crazy is that I believed him.'

'It's a bold plan, no doubt about that,' Matt said. 'And most people would have to say that it can't be done.'

Luke turned to the older man. 'Are you one who would say that?'

'Of course,'

'But you're in?' Luke asked a little uneasily.

'Oh, I'm in all right.'

'How come you're in then?'

'Well, I want to see what happens,' Matt told him. 'You know, like, I'd like to see how it all turns out.'

Steve nodded. 'There's more to it than that, right?'

'Huh? I suppose there is.' Matt nodded.

Mark shook his head and looked at Matt more closely.

'It is important', Steve said, turning more serious, 'that you are entirely aware of the fact that the expertise you possess individually is absolutely essential to the project as a team.' He paused for a moment to look carefully at each face before going on.

'And most important of all is trust. I had to know that I could trust you, and you had to know that you could trust me. And that trust extends further. It is a trust not only in the moral sense, but with what we are going to do, there has to be trust in the physical as well.'

There was a gap where no one said anything, each of them with their own thoughts.

Steve broke the silence with a measured few words. 'So that's it.'

Then it was quiet again, too quiet for the boyish-looking Luke. He shuffled around, waiting for someone to say something. Finally, it was Matt who asked what was probably on all their minds. A question that required an outright confirmation from Steve.

'So it's on?' he asked simply.

Steve answered the simple question with a simple answer. 'It is.'

'Well', Matt scratched the back of his neck, 'now don't get me wrong. Like I said, I'm in, all right, in all the way. But do *you* believe it can work?'

'Yes, Matt, I do,' Steve answered. 'It's on, and it's going to work.'

Matt scratched the back of his neck again. Then with an agreeable nod and a grin to go with it, said, 'All right then. On with the motley!'

Steve smiled for a moment or two then became serious again. 'You all know what you have to do, so for now, why don't we just shake on it and wish each other good luck in the enterprise we are about to undertake?'

And that's what they did. They shook hands, thereby demonstrably pledging themselves to the venture.

CHAPTER 2

Time and Motion

Miss Baxter glanced at the clock on the wall. Twenty seconds to nine. She picked up pad, pencils, and a neatly stacked pile of mail and printouts. She stood, moved to the inner office door, and placed her hand on the knob. And then Miss Baxter looked up. She could see Steve through the office complex, heading towards the glass door marked, 'TIME & MOTION', and below, in smaller lettering, 'Steve Wheeler'.

This office was still part of yet rather separated from the rest of the plush and tasteful paneled suites on the multi-departmental floor. To reach it, he walked almost the entire length of this upper level, acknowledging and returning as he did so the friendly greetings of the staff he encountered.

At the exact stroke of nine, he entered the outer office and went on through as his secretary adroitly opened the door.

'Good morning, Miss Baxter', he said softly. Without any loss of pace, he swept into his office with Miss Baxter following directly behind.

'Good morning, Mr Wheeler.'

The office wasn't all that big, but it was impressive in an executive-looking way. Much of the space, however, was taken up by all kinds of gadgetry and electronics concerning the study and operation of time and motion.

Steve took his seat at the desk as the efficient, middle-aged secretary placed the already opened mail before him. He straightaway pressed a button on the desk which illuminated and set in motion a desk clock recording the time elapsed in seconds and minutes.

Miss Baxter seated herself on the opposite side of the desk and opened her pad.

Steve glanced over the first letter and began to dictate: 'Johnston, Osborne, and Higbee, for the attention of Theodore Johnston, Sr. Dear Theo, I am most gratified to have received …'

He raced along at a constant high-speed pace, but the unflappable Miss Baxter's nimble shorthand was more than up to it. As one item was dealt with, there was no pause as he moved on to the next: 'And be assured, Mr Bushnell, we do appreciate your informing me that the time and motion systems we have instituted throughout your organization have met with approval and …'

The clock ticked off the minutes and seconds as Steve continued to dictate letters, emails, and memos. Neither seemed surprised when a soft buzzing sound sprang from the desk clock. Steve, without the least pause in his dictation, merely reached over to press a button, halting the irksome sound. '… be assured that your difficulties were fully recognized and, with your cooperation, reorganized in to the smooth operation that you now enjoy. Yours, etc.'

He turned over the last letter into a tray marked 'actioned'.

'All done', beamed Miss Baxter, 'and right on time too.'

'No, Miss Baxter. Right on time is precisely on time.'

'Well, almost on time. It was only a little over.'

'We were thirty seconds over. When time is organized to exactitude, a miscalculation of thirty seconds could mean failure to the motion.' He pondered on that for a few moments. 'Even disaster.'

The phone buzzed, and Miss Baxter picked up the instrument. 'Mr. Wheeler's office', she said in her secretarial tone. 'Very well.

Thank you.' Miss Baxter replaced the receiver. 'The group is assembled in the Taylor suite, Mr Wheeler.'

<hr />

Lime-finished oak panelling dominated the interior of the conference room. A few tasteful watercolors and photographs broke up the static woodwork, but nothing was highlighted that would detract from the purposes for which the room was intended: industrial or business lectures given by skilled spokespeople.

About twenty people sat facing a speaker's platform, chatting quietly to each other. Steve entered and walked quickly to a table upon which was a perking coffee pot. Quite suddenly, the pot tipped and poured steaming coffee into a cup at the precise moment Steve arrived at the table. He picked up the freshly poured brew and took a sip.

'Hmm, good coffee.' He smacked his lips lightly and went on. 'Time and motion can be applicable to anything, even the needs of the inner man.'

There were a few chuckles, and one man—to call him simply a little on the chubby side might be something of an understatement—started to applaud but stopped halfway through the second hand-slap when he became aware that he was alone in doing so.

Steve knew the coffee bit was not dazzling stuff, and he thought it was kind of corny. But it did serve a purpose. The clients liked that kind of thing when a moment of time and some sort of action are seen to be linked, thereby making a visual connection between time and motion.

'Good morning, everyone,' he continued. 'You, ladies and gentlemen, through the systems of time and motion that we have implemented for you can return to your organizations with the confidence that you now have a significantly smoother operation in the running of all aspects of your companies.' Steve took a short pause before going on. 'In addition to which, and just as important, secure in the knowledge that you are wholly prepared to cope with any problem that may arise. I know it, and you know it.'

There was a general amount of nodding and a soft murmuring of concurrence.

Steve had an easy-going style and a voice that carried well in a low-tenor pitch with what is now considered to be the mid-Atlantic accent. He leaned on the rostrum's paper holder and looked over his audience, comprised mostly of executive and managerial people. But there were others who perhaps one might not expect to find included in such a managerial type of group.

'Today', he continued, 'let us review during this, our final and somewhat condensed session, what we have learned in the past weeks. Motion study and time study, as you know, were the essential parts of the scientific management movement, which didn't really come into prominence until around the turn of the twentieth century.' Steve stepped away from the rostrum and walked around in front of his audience.

'An engineer by the name of Frederick Winslow Taylor pioneered the techniques of scientific management, and in 1881, while working for the Midvale Steel Company, he introduced time and motion study as a means of increasing efficiency. And it is certainly worth noting that he incurred considerable resentment from those affected by it.'

Steve walked over to the wall where a portrait of Frederick W. Taylor was prominently displayed. 'I suppose it is entirely understandable that he incurred so much disapproval in those days; they weren't ready for it. But there is no doubt about it, that was the start of time and motion.'

He moved closer to the painting of Taylor, folded his arms, and leaned against the wall for a moment or two. Then he turned abruptly to stroll to the opposite side of the room. All the while, his audience followed his movements, gestures, and the way he locked his eyes to theirs. No doubt they appeared to hang on his every word.

Steve was good at this stuff. He was, perhaps, a consummate master in this kind of setting.

'Motion study originated by Frank and Lillian Gilbreth.' He stepped up to a portrait of the Gilbreths and took up the arms-folded, wall-leaning posture. 'It was largely employed for the analysis and improvement of work methods. This, and time, are what we are concerned with here today.' He smiled openhandedly at his audience. 'The great expansion in business and industry over the years has brought with it a wider acceptance and greater use of motion and time study.'

The audience had heard all this before. And although Steve had the ability to make subtle changes to heighten interest, it was mostly his casual yet somehow dynamic get-up-and-go methodology which captivated them.

'Motion study, as defined by the Gilbreths, was the study of motions used in the performance of an operation or activity with the purpose of eliminating all unnecessary motions and building a sequence of the most useful motions to achieve maximum efficiency.'

He walked back to the rostrum, leaned his arms on it, and measured his listeners carefully. 'All of you here today have had studies made by our company of your various businesses to determine the most efficient use of time and motion in your individual situations.'

Steve looked keenly and directly at almost everyone in his audience, knowing his words would have a greater effect by making individual eye contact. His gaze quickly moved from one to another. A second or two with this man, more for that woman. Those singled out for added attention were a man sitting in the front row and the rotund, more working-class man in the back row. Both were most attentive, with the gentleman in front nodding enthusiastically from time to time. The man in back emphasized his keen interest by not moving a muscle except to follow Steve's movements as though mesmerized.

'In conclusion', Steve broadened the smile, 'I wish to emphasize that you must never deviate from the system we have set up, no matter what happens.' He made this last pronouncement forcefully. 'I feel that with the series of lectures you have attended and the plans which have been prepared, you will find escalating benefits from this experience.'

Again he surveyed them carefully. He let a few seconds pass for emphasis before concluding, 'Thank you for your kind attention.'

There was the usual gentle swell of applause which Steve acknowledged for a moment before stepping from the rostrum.

The listeners rose and crowded around him, shaking his hand along and offering their thanks and other appropriate remarks. The rotund man stepped up a little too quickly, thereby cutting off one of the others, an executive type who didn't take the cutting in line well and delivered the man a withering scowl of disapproval, which the man noted but promptly disregarded by roughly turning his back on him.

'Thanks, Mr Wheeler,' he said.

'No, no. Thank you, Mr Tubbs.'

The executive's eyes followed the man all the way back to his seat. Then he muttered, 'The churlishness of the working class I suppose. Oh well.' A smirk dropped instantly to be replaced with what passed for a smile. 'Anyway, thanks, Wheeler. I must say I was intrigued. Now I'm quite motivated. Yes, that's it, motivated. Our business has always been considered rather rigid, but now, with one or two innovations ... Well, one of the things I always tell our clients is that without expansion, you are standing still. I—that is, we—are considering expansion of ourselves. And another thing I always say to our ...' He was being pushed a little as there were trying to get in to have a few words with Steve. So he finally concluded, 'Ah, yes. Well, thank you Wheeler.' He shook Steve's hand stiffly.

'The pleasure is mine,' Steve said.

'Yes, yes. And you know, I see profit in this.'

'So do I, Mr Bishop, so do I.'

CHAPTER 3

Kate: More than Just Good-Looking

It wasn't immediately that Steve realized there were things that were unusual about this girl. Of course, first off, she was beautiful. But it wasn't just that. She was unlike any girl he had ever known—and Steve had known a lot of girls.

Pretty much every relationship begins with physical attraction, and there was no doubt about her attractiveness. She was a head-turning beauty. Her perfect light-olive skin was complemented by long, almost jet-black hair; straight, white teeth, and the most penetrating green eyes Steve had ever seen. Kate was a stunner, and he was attracted to her for those reasons. At first. She was perhaps not unique per se but certainly different.

But there was more to her than the fact that she was a natural beauty. She was, at the same time, quite self-effacing about being the knockout that she had to know she was. She had a strong and agreeable personality and was well educated and well spoken. Although in this regard, she divulged practically nothing of a personal nature. Oh, yes, she was open enough about the customary things that one says, but there was nothing really deep. Steve wondered if it was perhaps because she didn't really trust him.

On the other hand, Steve told her a lot about himself, his background, and his childhood. He encouraged her to respond in kind, but all he really found out about her were the basic things, nothing significantly personal. To be sure, she was not the kind of person one got to know easily. Not that he wanted to appear to be overly curious.

There was no question, he believed, that she had something on her mind. But even after they had been dating for some time, he was still very much in the dark as to who this green-eyed beauty really was.

Kate had a good job, appropriately in the cosmetics business, and she was always well dressed. Steve contented himself in the one thing of which he was sure: He could be in the company of this beautiful, highly intelligent girl almost anytime he wanted, and he wanted to be with her more and more.

And so it continued through the first weeks of their friendship. She, like a prisoner of war, her name, rank, and serial number were about all he knew about her.

He had known her for a little more than three months when one Friday, still quite early in the evening, his phone rang. It was Kate. Could he please come round to see her?

'Sure. What's up?'

'Can you come over now?'

'Sure. Is anything wrong?'

'Right now. Please.'

Kate opened the door and led him into the living room of her small, comfortable apartment. She asked him to take a seat but offered him no refreshment.

She began speaking quickly, in a clear, crisp manner, as though everything she was about to say had been thought out beforehand. 'I suppose you noticed that I haven't been very forthcoming.'

'I noticed.'

'Well, the thing is …' She paused for a moment and looked at him, as if deciding if she would talk openly or not. Apparently deciding that she would, she went on, 'I have learned not to trust anyone right off the bat. You must have noticed that, too, right?'

'I did.'

'Well, the thing is …' She paused again, looking at him carefully for a few awkward moments. Then she went on quickly as though if she didn't get it out, she never would. 'Oh, what the hell. I have a problem, and I think you might be able to help me with it.'

'Of course, if I can.'

'Thank you.' She sighed and began to speak more slowly. 'It's not a long story, really. I won't get into parts of it that you don't need to know so as not to waste your time.'

'Fine.'

'Okay, to begin, I was working in Hollywood and—'

'Hollywood?' he interrupted.

'Yes, Hollywood, and—'

'And you're from Minnesota, right?' he interrupted again.

'Yes, originally. Please don't interrupt.' It was a soft rebuke.

'Sorry.'

'The part I want you to know about is after I left Hollywood. I drove here from California, really not too long before I met you. At that time, I was in kind of a hurry to put as much distance between me and Hollywood as quickly as possible. Anyway, after I'd been on the road for a day or so, I began to slow down and take side roads.'

Steve nodded.

'I really don't know why I did that', she said in answer to some likely though unasked question.

She walked over to a small table, poured some whiskey into a glass, added a little ice, and handed it to Steve. He nodded his thanks, unspoken so as not to interrupt her train of thought.

'Anyway, I got off the interstate somewhere; I don't remember exactly where. I took secondary roads until I was passing through Kentucky. I just wanted to get away from everything that I had been doing, a kind of a solo road trip to clear my mind, I suppose. It seems a little crazy looking back on it. I decided to get back onto the interstate, and that's what I was trying to do when I found myself in this small rural area in West Virginia. It was really just a lot of rundown farmhouses and cowsheds. That's when it happened. There was this accident.'

Kate hesitated again and picked up the whisky bottle to refresh his drink, but he hand-motioned his thanks, but no. She took a sip from a glass of water.

'It was getting to be dusk, and I was on a dirt road that came to an end at the gate of a broken-down farmhouse. I thought of asking for directions, but the house was up an overgrown track, so I decided to turn around to go back the way I had come.' She paused. Steve had the feeling she was about to come to an unpleasant part.

'As I said, it was dusk and getting dark quickly, I didn't see anyone around, so I started to back up. Then I heard a loud noise.' She took a deep breath. 'I had run over a little girl.'

She was finally able to get it out.

'I guess I was mad at myself for getting lost like that and wasn't paying attention.' She looked at him closely for any reaction to this. There was none.

She went on to tell him how a man, presumably the father of the little girl, had appeared from somewhere. He quickly scooped up the little girl before Kate had time to get out of her car, placed her in the back seat of an old car, and rushed her off to a hospital. 'Go wait in the house!' he had shouted to her as he drove off. She saw several other people, women and kids, standing at the door. One of the women waved her inside. They were apparently some sort of farming family, and by the look of the house and it's old and mostly beat-up furniture, not exactly well-off farmers.

Of the other children in the house, it was easy to see they were not all from the one family. Some were older, more grown up. Others seemed way too young for the couple she assumed were the parents. But she thought maybe it was the hard life on the land that made these people just look older than they really were. Or maybe it was the way they all stared at her as though she was some kind of oddity.

Well, in a way, at the time she supposed she was an oddity. After all, they had not asked her to run over a member of their family, maybe hurting her badly or even, she remembered shuddering at the thought, killing her. She had wondered about the southern hospitality that she had heard so much about. No one had asked her if she'd like some coffee or anything.

The little girl was four years old, but she was not the youngest. There was one who seemed to be only about three who stared at her through the crack of a slightly opened door. For the most part, the folks left her alone at one end of what she presumed was the main room in the house, talking in undertones, which she had to suppose revolved around the accident.

After what seemed an eternity but was actually about half an hour, the man returned home. With him was another man, an older man, who seemed to be the head of the family.

Kate's insides tightened as she waited for him to tell her the condition of the child. The man ignored her. He went straight to a plate of food and began to eat leisurely while the rest of the family looked on. Kate, however, was not about to succumb to any southern family protocol and wanted to know right away how the girl was. The old man did all the talking. He told her that 'Josie was hurt bad.' How bad, she had wanted to know. What were her injuries? The man tortured her with ponderously slow replies to her urgent questions.

It turned out that her right leg was crushed. She had other minor injuries that would heal, but, 'That old leg is mostly squashed up pretty bad,' the old man had said coolly.

Kate had told him she could stay in a motel or a hotel and help in any way, but he told her that 'Wouldn't do no good', as the little girl was afraid of being in the hospital. Besides, he wouldn't let Kate go see her anyway, 'cause she's scared you'll come hurt her again', he had told her callously.

Kate told Steve that at that moment, she had two strong feelings, humiliation and animosity. A compelling sense of guilt for injuring a little girl, and utter distaste for this old man. He had made her embarrassment all the more acute with his cold-hearted attitude. It was an accident, after all. She hadn't meant to hurt anyone, much less a helpless four-year-old. Most of all, though, she had a great feeling of wanting to be away from this place.

Of course, she felt wretched for what she had done and would do anything she could to help. 'It's goin' to cost,' the old man had told her pointedly. Kate had said that naturally, she would pay any bills. She would also contact her insurance company. But he said, 'No. It would be okay if we take care of things between them.' Kate was about to write him a check but then thought better of it. Instead, she gave him all the cash she had with her, about $370.

The old man, who finally told her the family's last name, Hawkins, did not see her off the premises, so she had to stumble through the unfamiliar yard to find her way out to her car in the dark. Nevertheless, she felt tremendously relieved to be away from the Hawkins clan and on her way once more. It was after midnight before she got back on the interstate and found a motel.

Since then, Kate had been in touch with Mr Hawkins on a regular basis. Sometimes he called her collect for more money.

'That's what happened,' Kate said and sighed. 'That's it.'

'How much?' Steve asked.

'About five hundred.'

'Each time?'

'Yes.'

'For how long?'

'Four months.'

'Do you know how much all together?'

'Ten thousand.'

'Ten?'

'Maybe twelve.'

'You reported all this to your insurance company I suppose.'

Kate had alternated between sitting in a chair and pacing during the story of how the accident happened. Now she stood up and moved to another part of the room, further away from him and to another chair.

She looked at him and shrugged.

'So no?'

'No.'

Kate sat, staring at a small part of the carpet that did not quite reach the wall near the fireplace.

'I see,' Steve said softly. He could see the mind struggle that was ongoing within her. He moved over to stand close to her chair. 'No lawyer either, I guess.'

'No.'

Steve decided to wait until she was ready to talk more instead of burdening her with the obvious questions. So he returned to his chair and waited.

'I really don't expect you to understand,' she said, still staring at that little piece of carpet. 'To understand how stupid I felt at the time. It's not really like me. I guess I was lost at that time, and in more ways than just being highway lost. But I was the one who caused it and nearly killed Josie; that is her name. And once I paid him the first money, I just felt guilty as hell about it. And I still do.'

She excused herself and went into the kitchen. He heard water running and a glass clinking. Kate returned to the room and sat down. 'It's been getting to me the last few weeks.'

'Okay', Steve said after taking a deep breath. 'What do you want to do now? I mean about the accident.'

'Well, I'm not sure if this is right or if it will work. That's what I need your help with. I think I'd like to pay Mr Hawkins a lump sum. I know it's too late to contact the insurance company. Anyway, I feel obliged to do it. I have the money, so I'd like to get this thing off my back.'

'Okay. Let me think about it. I'll see what I can do.'

CHAPTER 4

Mr Hawkins

Steve left after Kate had told him how he could get in touch Mr Hawkins. He had already decided on what action he would take. The next day Steve caught an early morning flight to Tennessee, rented a car, and made a quick trip to the Hawkins's place. He was back in the city late that night.

He went over to see Kate right away.

'I have some news for you,' he said.

'Good or bad?'

'Some of both. Perhaps you'd better sit down. It's about Josie.'

Kate conjured in her mind a crippled little thing, helplessly bound to a wheelchair or on crutches for life through her carelessness. The glimpse she had at the time of the accident was too quick to penetrate her memory, and all she had for visions were the ones conjured up in her overworked imagination.

He could see where her thoughts were heading, so he spoke quickly. 'It was a scam, Kate.'

'What.'

'Yep, just a scam. And I'm afraid you fell for it. But don't get me wrong. Anyone would have.'

'But, I, I, the little girl, Josie.'

'There was no accident. Your car's rear hit the fence; that was the bang you heard. The kid was nowhere near your car. The man simply grabbed up the kid and took her over the grandad's house. Grandad, that would be the redoubtable Mr Hawkins. And that's where she stayed until you left. This old guy is like a legend back there. Been doing all kinds of shit like this all his life, and his two sons are the same. If you had reported it to the sheriff, they would have locked him up ... again. They're like the local two-bit crooks. I was only able to squeeze a little money out of him, the rest ...' Steve shrugged.

'Oh, for God's sake. What an idiot I am. I should have thought it might be a scam, but it really never entered my head. I was sort of knocked off balance in kind of a shock, I suppose. I guess I wasn't thinking clearly. All I could think of was this little girl lying broken in some hospital.' She sighed. 'Can you understand that?' she asked softly.

'Sure I can. That would be the natural reaction for anyone.'

Kate shook her head. 'Huh, a scam.'

'And about the money—'

'I don't care about the money,' Kate interrupted.

'That's good because there is no money. Well, practically none, nine hundred bucks, but ...'

'I don't want it, Steve. It would just remind me.'

'Okay. I understand.'

They stayed silent for a few moments as Steve let her soak it all up. Finally, Kate put her hands in his. 'Thank you,' she said softly.

'Forget it. Huh, that old man Hawkins is something else.' He laughed, but he knew it was not the time for talking about that. 'Forget it. And I mean forget it, the whole thing.'

He stood and held her close for a moment. She nodded silently, and he left. She didn't try to stop him; nor did she express further gratitude. All she felt was relief. That night, a great many thoughts ran through Kate's mind—this thing with the fake accident, of Roy, of her time in Hollywood. And trust. Could she trust anyone again? But that thought lasted less than a few seconds. Curiously, she felt the opposite. In fact, every part of her being would be strengthened by this and other things that had happened in her life. Her mind was never clearer. She smiled to herself. Her life was on track again. No, it was better than that. At last, her life was really on track. And there was someone she knew she could trust.

⁕⁕⁕

Steve hadn't told her the entire story about the scam. When he arrived, he made a few inquiries in the small town near where the Hawkinses lived. It wasn't hard to find out everything he needed to know before confronting Mr Hawkins. The general store, a farm equipment supplier, and finally, the town clerk at the mayor's office, it took him no more than a few minutes at each.

When he arrived at the Hawkins's place, he saw two children, a boy of about five or six years old, and a little girl around the same age. He walked over to them. 'Hello, Josie.'

The little girl looked at him curiously. She didn't speak but didn't seem to be afraid. It was the boy who spoke up. 'Huh? That ain't Josie,' he said in the know-it-all sort of way little boys have. 'That's Josie over there.' He pointed to another little girl, just rounding the side of the house, going hell for leather on a small tricycle. Steve walked over to her.

'Hey, Josie. How you doing?'

She jumped off the trike and ran up to the other two children, smiling. 'Just fine,' she said.

The front door of the house opened, and a heavily built man of about forty stepped out. 'What do you want?'

A tall, grey-haired man, who Steve presumed to be the oldest of the clan, followed him. He waved a hand that silenced his son. 'What can I do for you, mister?' Then he shouted, 'You kids get on round the back, you hear? And I mean right now!' They scooted away fast, Josie now pushing the tricycle.

'You must be Mr Hawkins,' Steve said.

'And I said, what can I do for you?'

'Little Josie looks pretty good.'

'What's it got to do with you? What the hell do want here anyway?'

'Twelve thousand bucks should do the trick, Mr Hawkins.'

'What the hell you talking about?'

'Oh, yes, of course,' Steve said pleasantly. 'It's about the scam you pulled about Josie's accident that never was. Shame on you, Mr Hawkins.' Steve tut-tutted. 'Well, we don't have to get into all that. Just get the money up, and I'll be on my way.'

'You the police?'

'Nope, just a collector.'

The old man smiled and called out loudly, 'Ellwood! You get on out here right now!'

'I guess you don't know how we treat collectors around here, boy.'

'Oh, I'd be careful if I were you Mr Hawkins.'

'You ain't me.'

'I'm asking you real nice. Please, Mr Hawkins, you don't want to do this.'

His smile growing larger as the seconds passed, the old man moved a little closer to Steve so as to face him head-on. Then his eyes shifted a little to his son. It was just a flick, but the signal was enough to send the big guy around to Steve's back. He quickly grabbed both Steve's arms at the elbows. And then he pulled him back tight into his chest. Steve relaxed.

'You know, stealing from young ladies isn't right, Mr Hawkins. Now if you'll just hand it over, the money that is, I'll be on my way.'

'You accusing me, boy?'

'I just want the money, Mr Hawkins.'

'Hold him good and tight there, Buck. Ellwood, get on over here. We're fixin' to have some fun,' he said with a toothy grin. 'You hold him tight there, Buck.'

Steve felt the strength of the big man holding him. And he was big. The grip tightened even more as Mr Hawkins was, with his ham-size fist, about to deliver a big roundhouse into Steve's midsection, a blow that would pole-axe a bull. And Steve knew that it would be followed by a whole lot more of the same. Steve assessed the situation instantly. He was someone who never looked for trouble of any kind, and certainly never a fight. But Steve knew how to fight. He believed that if you had to fight, you have to fight to win. Or more important, not to lose. And he knew that losing here would be really bad.

These were tough men, and Buck had him in an iron grip. But Steve knew that he could use that to his advantage. Mr Hawkins took a perfect position to start pummeling, pulling his arm back as if loading a canon. The came arm around, and the huge fist was on its trajectory to his midsection when Steve, at the same instant, lifted his feet one after the other, using the grip Buck had him as leverage in such a way that he exploited Buck's weight as well as his own. Steve unleashed a mighty right foot deeply and full force into Mr Hawkins's crotch. That was instantly followed by Steve's other foot into the same spot. It was a flash of movement, almost like a ballet dancer's move. It was executed so fast that it would be challenging to see when the first kick ended and the second found its mark. Steve exerted so much force that he was off the ground when he delivered the kicks. Courtesy of Buck's iron grip.

The old man's eyes almost popped out of his head with the immediate excruciating pain. His mouth opened, and the roaring sound of a great release of air came out as he went down.

Buck watched the old man fall, and in doing so, loosened his grip somewhat. As the old man had begun to deliver what would have been a devastating blow, Hawkins's other son, Ellwood, arrived on the scene and rushed to help Buck. But as things turned out, he actually hindered him, allowing Steve to swivel around and deliver a killer shot to Buck's overstuffed belly, followed instantly by a shot deep into his kidney and three hard right-hand punches to Buck's big face, one after the other in under than a second. Buck staggered backwards, and Steve moved in to let him have one more, a left to

Buck's right eye that would have to be stitched and would be black for weeks. Buck went down heavily into the dust.

Meanwhile, Elwood, had had the foresight to bring a long heavy axe handle to the party, and he took a mighty swing at Steve's head. Steve ducked. Elwood swung again, missed again, and lost the grip on the axe handle, and it flew—sadly landing with a mighty whack right between Buck's eyes as he was trying get up to rejoin the battle—knocking him out cold. Elwood charged at Steve, but Steve was way too quick, sidestepping the big man and belting him in both sides of his face with viscous rights and lefts.

It was over.

Old man Hawkins, Buck, and Elwood lay sprawled in the front yard dust while Steve checked out his hands. There was a little pain. There would be bruising later, but not that much. Steve knew how to hurt without being hurt. He went over to the old man, who had come to, more or less, but was making no attempt to get to his feet.

'Like I said, Mr Hawkins, you shouldn't be stealing from young ladies. That just isn't right,' Steve said, waving a finger in his face. 'But you were right about one thing. It sure was fun.'

⋯⋯⋯

Sitting there in the apartment, Steve thought about it. *Three years ago. Can it be three years? Well, like they say. time flies.*

He shook his head out of the reverie as she came into the room. He looked at her admiringly. 'Beautiful,' he said. 'It fits perfectly.' He stood and took a step back, so he could get the full effect of Kate from her flat black shoes to the top of her little red bonnet.

CHAPTER 5

A Train, a Bus, and a House

'Very nice, Mr Bloore, really, very nice,' Steve said as the elderly real estate agent led him down the wide staircase.

'I hope you'll be comfortable during your stay.'

'Oh, I'm sure of that,' Steve said as they entered a large formal drawing room through white double doors.

The house was set in an upper-class neighborhood five miles or so outside central Boston. It rented out to holiday makers, weddings, and such. It was a manor house, old but quite comfortable. There were seven bedrooms, most with attached bathrooms. On the lower floor were several spacious living rooms. The beautiful house was surrounded by a large formal garden with a long driveway leading from the street to the front door.

'Your copy of the rental agreement.' Mr Bloore handed him the one-sheet document. 'The house is yours for one month, or any part thereof.'

'Fine. Of course I explained I may not stay that long.'

'Perfectly all right. However, uh, hmm'. Mr Bloore coughed a little cough. 'There can be no refunds for a shorter stay, you understand.' He almost whispered the last part of the sentence.

'Oh, of course not, Mr Bloore. I wouldn't expect it.'

'Ah, very good,' said Mr Bloore, relieved the distasteful subject of money would not be an issue. 'Here are the keys.' He smiled. 'Enjoy your stay.'

Two delivery men entered the Italian-marbled foyer carrying one of the larger boxes. They placed it along with several others of the same type of varying sizes. One of the men approached Steve. 'There you go, sir. Seven boxes in all.'

He held the clipboard out. Steve signed it after glancing over to quickly count off the boxes stacked in the entrance hall. His tip to the trucker was generous but not ostentatious. The man thanked him and left.

Mr Bloore had a slightly bemused look on his face. 'I must say, you don't travel light.'

'Oh, just some pieces for an experiment I'll be working on.'

'Experiments! Oh dear. Nothing, ah, hazardous, I hope.'

'Oh, no, no.' Steve laughed at the very idea. 'Absolutely harmless,' Steve assured the elderly agent as he led him to the door.

'Well, let me wish you a pleasant stay. And, ah, I hope your experiment meets with success.'

'Oh, it will, Mr Bloore, it will.'

'Here it is, Matt. This is us, car E.'

New York's Grand Central Station is always busy. Folks arriving and departing, coming from somewhere or going to somewhere, or simply using the building for easy access to the streets surrounding the station as it is plunked right there in mid-Manhattan. This day there seemed to be even more people, no doubt because it was nearing the Christmas holidays, and the pace was picking up.

'Fine. In you go, Luke,' Matt replied.

Although the railway car was already crowded, they found their seats easily. Matt swung Luke's baggage into the overhead rack, followed by his own accompanied by two noisy grunts.

The railway porter checking his way down the car moved in to help. 'You gentlemen okay here?'

'Sure thing. Thanks,' Matt said genially.

'You just let me know if you need anything.'

'Thanks, we're fine,' Matt replied.

⁕⁕⁕

Although the bus was standing there and the driver was in his seat, it seemed to be one of the added annoyances of the Port Authority that passengers must stand in line until almost the very last minute to board and then push and shove each other into the vehicle, handing their tickets to the essentially man-of-few-words driver.

The Port Authority building itself can be a house of horrors at times, but holiday seasons seem to bring with it the worst in people, all in a hurry to get somewhere. Johnny and Mark found two seats near the middle of the bus. Almost immediately, the bus backed out of the loading platform and maneuvered out of the building.

'You want to know something, Johnny?' Mark asked, settling into his seat.

'Yeah, what?'

'I like buses.'

'Uh huh.'

'No, seriously, old boy. I really like to sit and relax.'

'I said, uh huh.'

'Yes, I can relax in a bus.'

The bus quickly found its way to the highway. It picked up speed but then settled into a smooth ride.

'Relax, huh?' Johnny countered, trying to get his long legs into an acceptable position. 'This, my friend, is not relaxation.'

'Oh, yes, relax, and watch the towns and country go by. That's relaxing.'

Johnny turned, cupped his chin in the palm of his hand, and wound up the relax or not relax topic with a succinct, 'I'm closing my eyes now.'

Mark shrugged and murmured to himself, 'Sleep. Yes, that's relaxing.' He turned back to the window and started to hum. After a moment, the hum turned into a song, softly, of course.

Johnny groaned. 'Jesus, he's a singer.'

'Oh yes. In the school choir from age eight to twelve,' Mark said as he took up the song again.

'What kind of song is that?'

'It's a wonderful old piece. It's a madrigal.'

'A mad what?'

'A madrigal. They're very old. Some people call them dithyrambs.'

'Oh, that. Why didn't you say that in the first place,' Johnny said in Brooklyn-accented sarcasm. Mark went on undeterred.

'Quite difficult to sing.'

'Yeah, well it ain't no *Top of the Pops* to listen to either.'

Ignoring the crack, Mark went on thoughtfully. 'Lovely melodies from long ago.'

'Hmm, maybe it would be better if it were song in the key of shut the fuck up.'

'Ah, not of a musical bent, eh?' Mark asked good-naturedly.

'Eyes closed.'

'You'd like it.'

'Eyes still closed.'

'Really, old boy, music is food for the soul.'

'Still closed. And what's this "old boy" shit?'

'Inoffensive, friendly expression.'

'Still closed.'

Two hours later, the train pulled to a soft halt into the station alongside the ironwork legend with the name on the city emblazoned over a metalwork flyover. Not too long after, the bus pulled into the terminal building with the hissing of air brakes and a loud squeal of rubber.

The driver turned to face his passengers and made a single word announcement: 'Boston!'

In the evening of the day after their arrival, Steve took a seat in the drawing room and waited for the others. Except for the alcohol ban, it was a fine dinner, and Matt said it was, several times. Steve had made up the menu, and the catering company delivered it to the house exactly as ordered. As planned by Steve, the four men left New York the previous day, travelling by different transportation modes and arriving at different times. Steve arrived at the house the day before the others by way of a large van he drove.

Leaving the dining area, the others assembled in the drawing room with Steve. Johnny and Mark bantered more amicably than they had on the bus, while Matt was telling Luke stories about the best and worse meals he had ever eaten, returning to the point that tonight's meal fell into the best category.

'Would you all take a seat, please?' Steve said.

The men arranged themselves comfortably in chairs and sofas, more or less facing Steve, who sat in a high winged lounge chair. He waited until they were settled and the joshing between Mark and Johnny waned, and Matt had come to the end of his gastronomic tales.

Steve looked them over for a moment or two before speaking. 'I trust you are all well rested?'

'Fine, couldn't be better,' replied Mark.

'Terrific!' This from Luke.

'Enjoyed the dinner?'

'I was just saying to young Luke here, one of the best I've eaten,' answered Matt.

31

'Good. Yes, good. Is there anything else? I mean, do any of you want anything else?

They looked at each other. Most of them just shook their heads. Matt said, 'I'm fine.'

'Okay,' Steve said. 'It starts tonight.'

Steve looked carefully at each of them. There was no real reaction to what Steve had just said; nobody said anything. Mark and Johnny remained relaxed. Only Luke sat up a little straighter, and a nervous smile appeared on his boyish face. Matt sat quietly, composed. The silence continued for a few more moments until Matt murmured, 'Okay then.'

Steve went on. 'Everything is set and timed to the second. From this time on, we will operate strictly in accordance with the operation and timing of the plan.'

Another pause.

'Are there any questions or comments?

They looked from one to the other, but there were no questions. Steve knew that they would feel a little jittery—they should. That was natural and expected.

'Very well,' he continued. 'We've gone over this many times. Just a last reminder: Nothing is to be brought with you, not a coin, not a stamp, a scrap of paper, absolutely nothing. You will wear the clothes provided right down to footwear. Not one personal item. Nothing. You bring nothing.'

Two hours and seventeen minutes later, Steve inspected the men, now kitted out in dark-blue overalls, including himself. He looked each man over carefully.

'All right, we leave here in exactly,' he checked his wristwatch, 'twelve minutes.'

CHAPTER 6

The Boston Water-Pumping Station

The huge four-storey municipal facility was decorated in the over-elaborate style of more than a century ago. Ornate gargoyles and water cherubs surrounded the high beams and pillars to make it appear as though these mythical creatures were holding the walls and ceiling in place. More columns and pillars arched high and over to meet in the middle of the building were also decorated with similarly detailed sculptures of florae and figures. Eerie and shadowed, the station looked more like an underground medieval cathedral than a municipal water works.

Six grand turbines stood regimentally in two rows. In the exact center was another huge piece of machinery. At floor level, the old bright work was patently striking, its enormous brass wheels and gauges polished to the nth-degree, while the shiny floor reflected the great columns and beams that stood as though haughty sentinels. A large altar-like granite block came up from the floor at the north end of the building. It held a bronze plaque with steel lettering that boldly proclaimed:

Boston Water Pumping Station
Opened July 1, 1899

A few of the pumping-station workers were engaged in a range of jobs such as checking gauges and turning switches and wheels. Other workers stood by, awaiting orders. Orders that would be delivered concisely by the man in charge.

At seven minutes to midnight, the man in charge positioned himself at a huge stopcock wheel located on the main control panel. He checked his pocket watch with the huge, white-faced Elgin clock on the wall. Nodding his head to the movement of the seconds for a moment, he then stood quite still and called loudly, 'Stand by!'

The men stood ready and focused.

'All right,' he shouted over the turbines' hum. 'Everyone to his station.'

This command was followed by a general scurry. Quickly all the men were standing at their designated positions, awaiting further orders.

One of them leaned over close to another. 'Hey, Mack, I'm still kind of new here, so let me ask you something.'

'Okay, but keep your voice down. He's got ears like a fox.'

'This thing tonight only happens every now and again, right?'

'Right. Every other day the job goes on as usual.'

'Yeah, I get that, but why does he do that himself? You know, the big wheel an' all.'

'Who knows?'

'Yeah, but …'

'Look, he's a prissy asshole. Don't ask.'

The new man shrugged. 'Okay.'

'I've been here nine years. He's changed some things that make no sense. I mean, what the hell difference does a few minutes either way matter? It's all bullshit.'

'Cut the chatter over there!'

'Yes sir,' the old hand answered. Then under his breath, 'See, ears like a fox, that's what he's got. The asshole!'

'Keep your eyes on those dials!'

At exactly midnight, the sound of a bell rang through the building. He had replaced his pocket watch and now turned the wheel furiously, while others threw electrical switches and checked metres. Slowly the arrows on the gauges began to wind down, and the turbine's hum began to diminish.

Deep under the pumping station, in the huge water tunnels, great iron gates closed slowly from both sides, cutting off the torrent of water that was powering through them.

'Report!' he shouted, 'Circuits one and two—the pressure reading?'

'Dropping fast.'

'Secondary channels?

Shouted replies came back different from areas of the building over the hum of the diminishing machinery noise.

'Checking three—dropping.'

'One dropping fast. Number one metre reads ninety pounds!'

'Number two reading seventy-eight and falling!'

'Very well,' he called back, his eyes fixed on the gauges in front of him. 'Three?'

'Number three, eighty and falling.'

One by one, the men reported gauge readings and other information. With the last of the reports called in, the cut-off was complete. The humming of the turbines drained down to silence, as did all the general machinery sounds of moments before. The many dials were now reading zero. In a place where the constant noise of machinery was routine, the roaring sounds diminished to an uncanny silence.

The boss stood very still and listened to the nothingness for several minutes. Satisfied shouting was unnecessary now, he called, 'Leave stations', in a quieter voice everyone in the building could still hear clearly.

The men finished locking off the machinery and moved back behind the iron safety railings.

'What happens now?' the new man wanted to know.

'Now we're off until six. It's the only time that the station is closed completely in the entire year. Then he will have us turn everything back on. Six hours from now, on the dot.'

The workers began to leave. The boss stood by the door as the men, all with heavy coats or jackets now, began to pass him. After looking over his domain, he lit a cigar. He was not satisfied until the end of it glowed red hot and sent smoke drifting up to the high ceiling. One more careful scan of the station, and he stepped through the opening. The old hand was right behind and about to pass him on to the outside of the door when the boss stopped him, barring his way with a huge arm. 'You', he said.

'Yeah?'

'You want to keep your job?'

'Sure.'

'Then keep your trap shut.'

'Yes, Mr Tubbs.'

CHAPTER 7

Zero Hour Minus Fifty Hours

A small strip of clear material appeared in the door jamb a few inches above the lock. Slowly it rocked back and forward, all while sliding downwards until it reached the spring bolt. A little pressure on the bolt section, and the door swung open. Luke entered first, closely followed by Johnny, Mark, and Matt. Steve was last and closed the door behind him. They stood for a moment or two, viewing the pumping station from inside the railing. Then Steve moved to the head of the line, stumbling slightly under the weight of the two large sacks he lugged.

They all carried what seemed to be more than they should be able to handle. Even the tiny Luke had a great sack strapped to his back and one in his arms. Once down the few steps and onto the floor of the station, Steve led them between the turbines to the west side of the building.

Protruding from the floor were six steel hatches. Steve checked them against the written plan he carried with the numbers of the hatches. He found the hatch he wanted almost immediately at the end of the row.

'This one,' he said.

Johnny put his load down and began turning the hatch wheel. The hatch resembled the type and size of hatches found on submarines. Under his strong urging, the wheel turned several revolutions, and the hatch opened. He swung it wide to reveal a steel ladder leading down. Kitted out in blue coveralls as they were, they completed their attire by putting on miners' hardhats with lights attached.

For a few moments, they stood in a circle and looked down into the darkness that they were about to enter. Matt shook his head and grinned. 'So far, so felonious,' he said softly.

'So far,' Mark agreed.

'Let's go,' Steve murmured. He tapped Johnny on the shoulder who, without a second's hesitation, descended by way of the twelve-foot steel ladder. He was closely followed by Mark, who had, in turn, received the shoulder tap from Steve.

The men on top began lowering the sacks of equipment that included two heavy gas cylinders. When all the equipment had been sent down into the tunnel, Luke went in—after a deep breath and a look of resignation. Matt followed quickly, murmuring under his breath, 'A for a leap in the dark.'

Steve, the last to enter, lowered himself into the blackness, carefully pulling the hatch cover back into position. Johnny took his place turned the inside wheel to relock the hatch until it was tightly sealed. The pumping station returned to its eerie silence.

One after another, the men switched on the light attached to each of the steel helmets. Except for that bright, concentrated lighting from the miner's headgear, they were in total darkness.

The tube they were in was eight feet in diameter and evenly curved. It was wet in the there, and although the air smelled of nothing they could put a name to, it was not unbreathable. Even though only a little water lay on the floor of the tube, the walls were dripping and flashed bizarrely as the helmet lights bounced off the damp on the steel. The beams, bobbing and weaving as they did with the movement of the men, made for an unnerving environment that had a discomforting effect on all of them except Matt, who seemed to be completely at ease.

'Okay, you work in pairs,' Steve reminded them. 'That way you'll find it much quicker to assemble the carts. Matt with Luke and Mark and Johnny, okay?'

'Right', Mark replied. 'You know I can't count the number of times we've been over all of this, Steve.'

'Yes, that's true. But we have to keep to the routine so that there are no misunderstandings.'

They began to put together four sturdy, aluminum hand trucks. *This is taking a little longer,* Steve thought, *than it probably should.* He made a mental note of it as he consulted a book on the pages of which were what looked like a jumble of figures and graphs. But they were, in fact, intricately detailed diagrams and numbers.

When the were assembled, the men placed the equipment on the rugged hand trucks. Steve attached a wheeled instrument to the lead truck and punched some numbers into it. When fully loaded, it was hard to believe the five men had carried all that equipment. It was little wonder they had staggered under the weight and bulk.

'Can we talk down here?' Luke whispered. 'I mean, can anyone hear us?'

'Sure. You can talk as loud as you like. No one can hear, no matter what we do. But,' Steve cautioned, 'while talking is okay, we should avoid doing any other unnecessary things. We are going to need our strength.'

He went to the lead truck and turned on a small but brilliant headlight, illuminating the great tunnel all the way to the first bend. 'We use only one light at a time,' Steve told them. 'So switch them on for the test, and then turn them off.'

They did as told. At the same time, Steve made one last check to see that everything was the way it should be. By the light of the truck, they could make out the intense expression on his face. 'Ready?'

No one said anything, indicating that they were ready. 'Okay then. Let's move.'

And the long march began.

'Just like a movie I saw once,' Luke said, a little nervously. 'Death in the sewers of London.' Since they were walking single file, Luke sensed rather than saw them looking at him in the anomalous half-light. 'I mean, there's no way out, is there?'

'Mark, you want to move up here now?' Steve called over his shoulder. Luke was third in line, behind Steve and Mark. Matt bought up the rear.

Luke mumbled to himself, 'Shit, what the hell are we doing down here anyway?' It was a mumble, but it was loud enough for Matt to hear what he said.

'Cheer up, Luke,' Matt said with a lightness to his tone of voice. 'I'll tell you what we're doing down here. We're on our way to …' he paused, delivered Luke a reassuring slap on the shoulder, and with a broad grin on his face chortled tunefully, 'to rob a nice old lady.'

CHAPTER 8

Hurray for Hollywood

Kate would probably still be living happily in Circle Pines, Minnesota, if she hadn't won a beauty contest. Maybe married to a dentist or a teacher, with a growing brood of kids. Or not married. Perhaps she would have become a teacher herself. After all, she was an honor student in high school and college, majoring in business administration and minoring in dramatic art.

Her college education was paid for in part by a dramatic arts scholarship she earned. But drama was something she thought of as more of a recreational thing than any serious idea that she might have a career in acting. The laws of probability told her that she would stay where she was, while her natural instincts and sense of adventure told her otherwise.

Her mother had died more than two years before. That was probably another reason her plans changed. Even though her mother's passing was not unexpected because of a long illness, it threw her into a state of flux for a while. But that did not last. And anyway, Kate never had any doubts that she would finish college because that was what her mother wanted for her more than anything.

However, the laws of probability would not win out this time. Her life to follow was profoundly changed when she won the beauty contest she was more or less talked into entering by friends. Winning made her eligible for the state finals of the Miss America competition.

And in part of the country renowned for the beauty of its women, it was no mean achievement to get that far.

Kate was beautiful and just the type judges like in beauty pageants. She didn't win, but she made it to the final four. That brought her to the attention of a television producer, who sent her photo and other details to a friend, an executive at a television company situated in one of the studios in Hollywood. He was impressed enough to offer her a screen test. It was expenses paid, so Kate had nothing to lose and considered it as a chance for an unexpected short vacation from her current job at a local beauty parlor. Never did she think it would really amount to anything. In this, she was not even half right.

The company liked the test and gave her a small part in a movie that was already in production. The actress Kate replaced had, for some reason Kate was never told, left the picture. In any event, here was this beautiful, twenty-three old girl, pretty much fresh from college with a degree in business administration, working as an actress in the mecca of the movie industry, Hollywood.

And Kate was indeed a beauty. With that long, raven-black hair and a flawless, lightly bronzed complexion, she photographed well. She did not, however, possess the high cheekbones directors and producers seemed to search endlessly for. No, hers was a more classic face, well moulded with just the suggestion of a dimple or two, and a high forehead. The main feature of her beauty, most people would have to agree, was her clear green eyes. If she wished, they could be as penetrating as a laser or as soft as a child's. Five feet seven inches tall, her figure was not even narrowly off perfect.

Rare also in that with just the touch of make-up and an inclination one way or the other, she could look the sophisticatedly glamorous type or a fresh, wholesome, vivacious, country girl. Or again using make-up techniques ever so slightly, boosted with flashing eyes, a wild spirit.

That her physical range was apparently unlimited was pleasing to the producers and directors who saw her during those first weeks in Hollywood. Her future looked bright.

Above all things, Kate was a realist. She knew, for instance, that she was no great actress and never would be, partly because she had little natural talent for acting. She didn't have what is sometimes called the 'X factor', that indefinable talent that can't be taught. She thought it rather silly some people could possibly think that she might be able to really act. She certainly was not, and would never be, another Katharine Hepburn, and she knew it.

Was it enough, she wondered, to get by with a pretty face and a nice figure? Oh sure, the dramatic classes at college were excellent, and she was a good student. She won that scholarship, after all. But this was Hollywood.

"So", she told herself during those first few weeks, "I'll go along with it as long as it suits me. But the minute these people realize I'm not an actress and never will be, I'll quit before making a fool of myself."

One of the first things to happen to anyone who becomes even moderately successful in the film capital is that they acquire an agent. In Hollywood, it is impossible to find an agent to represent you unless you are already working. Yet, you probably can't work unless you have an agent; it's a catch-22. But if you get a job on your own, what happens? An agent will suddenly appear—like the flu.

Ah, the agent. Essential, lower-end actors would be willing to confirm. But invisible and unavailable when most needed, most hard-working actors would agree. Kate was introduced to Marty Steinman during her first week, and he would become her agent before the second. Marty found her an apartment in one of the complexes inhabited by writers, actors, and other film people at what she thought was a fairly reasonable rent.

It was in the Hollywood Hills, overlooking Burbank, Warner Bros. and Universal Studios. Lincoln Films was located on the Burbank lot where she was doing her first picture, so she could easily walk down the hill from the apartment in only ten minutes. She determined, however, that should she remain for any length of time in Hollywood, she would move to an even more reasonable and desirable place to live. Her salary was not very much during that first job, but Marty had lined up what he called 'hot prospects' for several more acting assignments.

These were small parts, not even what are called 'bits'. But each came with a modest increase in her pay rate. He also arranged her application for union membership in the Screen Actors Guild. And one last thing. He convinced her that she had to change her name. 'Absolutely everybody does it,' Marty told her. 'Kate Martin is not a screen name. Doesn't have a ring to it. You get it? No ring!'

In the end, after sorting through a number of possibilities and making sure the name was not already taken by another actor, they settled on a moniker that was acceptable to Marty and with which Kate would feel comfortable. So Kate Martin became Catherine St. Claire.

By the time Kate had been in Hollywood for almost two years, she had done small parts and bits in four films, a featured part in two episodes of one of a TV action series, and a commercial for a nationally advertised brand of beauty product. The commercial was what brought in the most money to her, and she was able to save regularly from it as well as buy herself a new sporty, compact car. But she stayed on in her apartment during the first year, vowing that this month would be her last each time she paid the rent.

Most actresses and actors are looking for either a really big part in a movie or an ongoing, hopefully starring, role in a television series. But Kate was not a dreamer, like the legion of actors, wanabees, and even veterans ever hoping for the one part that would rocket them to stardom.

And just like so many others with equally bright prospects at first, Kate's star had not risen. The real possibility of continuing in small, unnoticed pieces seemed likely to be as good as it would get. Since nothing of any real significance developed, Kate could see that the best she could hope for was to keep trying for a part in a series, as well as to continue auditioning for parts in what were, to be honest, mostly forgettable films.

Her social life was less than assertively active. However, Kate had made a number of friends in about the same situation as herself, actors struggling for bigger parts but surviving with the work they could get. She also became acquainted with several of the writers and tech people who also lived at the same apartment complex or who she encountered at agencies, studios, and auditions.

Kate also met her share of oddballs and outright kooks. But there were some nice people too. One of the more agreeable people she had met and become friendly with Diane, who worked as an extra.

Diane was maybe one of the most beautiful young women Kate had ever seen. She had *the* look, the real American girl next door. And she was really nice. On the job or on her own time, she was friendly and instantly likeable. She had darkish blonde hair, a lovely face, and the bluest of blue eyes. Kate knew she, herself, was, let's face it, good-looking, but she was just like any number of the girls who came to Hollywood. Diane, on the other hand, was exceptional. Yes, there was no doubt. Diane was drop-dead gorgeous. Kate figured she was about nineteen or twenty. But with the right costume and make-up, she could register older or younger. Whatever was wanted for the show.

Just as much as the scenery, all movies and TV shows need extras. Without them, the screen would be barren and flavorless. Diane had been in hundreds of movies and TV shows—in a crowd, walking into or out of a shop, high school or college shots in the classroom or on a campus, in an office, or just as background to the featured actors.

Diane had turned up for a crowd scene or some office shot on the same set as Kate a few times, and now and then, they chatted during the frequently long spells between takes. Nothing of any importance, just the regular chit-chat. They had coffee and talked together a number of times, and Kate liked her. Who would not? She was a really nice girl.

This time, however, Diane began talking about herself, and she told Kate something that almost floored her. When Kate asked her how long she had been in Hollywood, Diane replied, 'Oh, a long time.'

'Can't be all that long.'

'Because I'm so young, you think. Right?'

'Yes.'

Diane smiled. 'How old do you think I am?'

'Oh, I don't know, eighteen, twenty?'

'I'm thirty-nine years old.'

'What? Are you kidding me? You look eighteen.'

Diane laughed. 'Yeah, I know. I've been working as an extra for twenty years.'

'Twenty years! I can't believe it, Diane. You look so young and fresh and well, you know what I mean.'

'Yeah, that's how I keep working.'

Kate shook her head. 'You could be, I mean did you ever—'

'I know what you're going to say,' she interrupted. 'Be an actor, right?'

'Yes.'

'The thing is, I can't act, can't fire at all. Gave it a shot at first, but I just have no talent for it.'

'But …'

'No Kate. Look, this is how it is. First, as an extra, I'm never out of work. I'm one of those extras that they want. There are a few of us who work all the time, but just a few. The rest, well, they more or less get by. About acting gigs, I used to get asked if I wanted a bit part or to try out for something bigger. Now they know I can't act, so they don't ask. That's fine, believe me. I'm reliable, and I get paid better than scale rate. And like I said, I'm always working. The thing is, I'd rather be an in-demand extra than a failed actress.'

Kate sighed. 'Wow, beautiful and smart.'

'Thanks. Yes, I could try for bigger things, but I know what I can't do and what I can. And another thing, I don't have to get involved with the big shots, most of whom are total assholes in every sense.'

'H'mmm, I guess,'

'Don't get me wrong, Kate. There are some good people here, no doubt about it. But like I said, most of them are assholes. The Hollywood game is all smoke and mirrors and bullshit.'

'Hollywood! Jesus, is anything real?'

'Not much.'

'You sure know your way around. Is that because you've been here and doing this for so long?'

'I suppose so. Another thing, I keep out of the way mostly. Listen, Kate, do you mind if I tell you something.'

'Of course not. What is it, Diane?'

'I survive here because I keep to myself, and I'll tell you why. The bosses are pigs, and those underneath them are toadies. And if you get mixed up with either of them, you're in trouble.'

'Okay?'

'I'm just saying to be careful.'

'Thanks, Diane. I will.'

'Yep, that's Hollywood.' Diane laughed for a moment. Then she looked at Kate with those blue eyes. 'I'll tell you something else that will surprise you. Something you might find hard to believe given that I've been in Hollywood so long.'

That made Kate laugh. 'Oh, I don't think so. There's no way you can surprise me more than you have.'

'Guess again, Kate. I'm a virgin.'

⁂

Kate was often invited to parties and events around Los Angeles, but she did not accept every invitation. Nor did she date anyone in particular, finding actors to be mostly interested in themselves with

47

'in looks' rather that 'outlooks'. And she repelled the usual hustle put on her by many of them.

She would occasionally, however, go to dinner or something with someone. The routine was becoming a little tedious, and by the time her third year in Hollywood was coming into view, she wondered how long she would keep doing this. Then two things happened at once.

First, Marty was able to sign her for a pilot in a new television series which, if picked up for the next season, might put her on the acting map and make her financial future secure. And second, she met Roy Delahunt.

The pilot rated quite high in the Nielsen's and was well received both by the sponsors and the general viewing audience. So the network picked it up for the next season. Kate had a more-or-less regular female role playing not quite opposite the star, who in the story was a private detective, but as his assistant and secretary. It was not a big part, but it was a good part, and Kate knew it. The detective was only seen in the office for short but regular periods, so it meant that she would have limited screen time. But it was a good job.

Even though it was as permanent an acting job as one could ever expect to get in Hollywood, nothing had happened to change her viewpoint regarding her own acting ability. Nor did she love the Hollywood scene that much.

The attraction was the money, several thousand dollars a week plus residuals. To her mind, it was a huge amount for so little talent, and she thought it even worse that the star would receive an obscene amount of money for each show. About her own salary, she thought, *Oh, well, that's showbiz.* If they were crazy enough to give it to her, she rationalized, she was smart enough to take it.

Roy Delahunt was in the middle order of Hollywood big shots. One way or another, he had interests in some TV shows that were produced by mostly independent companies, but he also had some involvement with the networks. The rap on him was that he had produced two or three modestly successful independent movies, been married twice, and was now paying large alimony in two directions and child support for one offspring. Or was it two? Depended on who said what.

He lived in the obligatory large house in the equally obligatory Beverly Hills part of Los Angeles and was an admitted forty years old. He was very good-looking. Wild streaks of grey ran through his thick, black hair. A well set-up body, coupled with a never stop energy, made him one of the studio somebodies on sight. Loudmouth Marty introduced them at Delahunt's request during filming of the pilot.

Although he had no financial interest in the show, Delahunt made it his business to know most things that were going on at the studios. His staff was well trained and enthusiastic in studio spying, reporting any details they could glean on new productions, deals, and contracts, along with summaries on any new talent.

He was interested, so he made a point of casually dropping in on the set. He was impressed with Kate's good looks and had asked the agent to introduce him. Marty did so with just the right amount of brown-nosing. Roy Delahunt was a big shot, and Marty was a low-end agent. They both knew were they stood on the Hollywood ladder.

Delahunt's polite but summary dismissal of the agent right after the introduction indicated the disregard he held for lower-scale agents. But Marty took no offence. He knew that was how big men treated little men in Hollywood. One day he hoped to be a big shot himself and be able to do the same thing to others on a lower rung. In doing so, he would not be relishing in any revenge. No, it was just the way it was in Hollywood. In his introduction, Marty enumerated some of Mr Delahunt's film and TV credits to Kate, who he hoped would appear suitably impressed. But it was really just to kiss the big man's ass.

In the short conversation between Delahunt and Kate that followed, he was charming and made himself easy to talk to by keeping the topics light and general. Kate was impressed by his easy-going style. In response, Kate was polite and pleasant.

Before he left the set a few minutes later, he invited her to a screening and cocktails at his house in Beverly Hills. He let it casually drop that it would be attended by several other guests, obviously to put the newcomer at ease.

She hesitated a little before accepting, but finally did so. Not because she saw Marty hovering on the other side of the stage, pretending no interest, but because she was genuinely impressed with Delahunt's charm and unruffling demeanour, not playing the Hollywood big shot that, by Marty's behavior, she could perceive he obviously was.

The affair was, as promised, attended by others, more than fifty people. A couple of Kate recognized as real big shots of the Hollywood scene, one or two of the older executives and their wives, but there were some familiar screen faces in attendance, too, but not the superstar variety. Rather, they were the successful journeymen people, actors and actresses who seem to be in every major motion picture, adding their capable support to the big names or superstars. Without these well-known professionals most film projects would flop.

There were also a few television stars present. They were the most recognizable and, at the same time, the most subdued in the company of those who could possibly determine the length of their film popularity and the strength of their financial futures.

Kate enjoyed the cocktails and conversation, but not the film; it was just a stretched-out trailer presenting a lot of action mixed in with a few dramatic scenes, a demo, really, of what it would look like when it became a movie. Some people applauded quite loudly and made complimentary remarks to Delahunt, pointing out that this or that shot or piece of action had appealed to them. Kate wondered if she had watched the same preview—or whatever it was.

After the what amounted to be a puffed-up preview was screened on the biggest screen Kate had ever seen outside a movie theatre, she wondered if it might be time to start thinking about leaving.

Delahunt had, on her arrival, introduced her to a group of people and then left her alone for the rest of the evening. People began to circulate, and a number of guests moved from the sumptuous living room, which had become a theatre for the evening, to the large terrace and pool area. Kate was about to do the same. So, after saying politely refusing a drink from the waiter, she was on her way to the open French doors when Delahunt came over to her.

'Well, Kate', he said and smiled, 'what did you think of it?'

She wasn't sure if she felt flattered or flustered that he remembered her name. 'Is it your film, Mr Delahunt? I mean, I didn't see your name on the credits.'

'Just on the financing side of the things. So, what did you think?'

'Well, you see, Mr Delahunt', she began, 'I don't know all that much about—'

'It's pure shit, isn't it?' he interrupted, followed up with a laugh.

She looked at him curiously before answering. 'Oh, I don't know. The people here seemed to like it.'

'Maybe some of them. Well, it is low budget.'

'But won't you lose money if it's no good?'

'I had a little to do with financing; I didn't say I put any money into it. As a matter of fact, I've already made a profit on it.'

'I guess I'll never understand this business.'

'Don't try,' he said quietly. 'You don't have to. You just need to know what you have to do in your job, which is acting. Just show up, and do the best job you can.'

'Thank you. That's good advice. I mean in acting, I'm still pretty new, and I need all the help I can get. Anything else?'

'Sure. Just one. Always go with your first instinct.'

'And?'

'There is no and. Trust your first instinct. If you feel it, go with it.'

'Well, to be honest—'

He cut her off. 'Honest? Huh! Listen, Kate, you're in the land of make-believe. Honesty has nothing to do with anything out here. It's just a whole lot of horse shit.'

They don't call it Hollywierd for nothing, she thought. 'Mr Delahunt, it sounds like you hate it.'

'Call me Roy. Hate it? Oh, no, honey.' He laughed. 'I love it.'

CHAPTER 9

Who Are You?
Who Am I?

There followed a period of several weeks between the pick up of Kate's show and the commencement of the actual production while scripts and sets were being prepared. It was a time when Kate had little to do besides show up for occasional meetings at the studio or for interviews with reporters and columnists. Those were set up by the publicity department for release later, when the show was being aired. There were some photo sessions, but the rest of the time was her own.

She saw quite a lot of Roy Delahunt during this period, attending screenings and one or two parties. It wasn't like a date; it was a mix of business and social, and always with groups of others in the industry. He never asked her out on an actual date. Kate wondered about that, and she wondered what she would say if he did.

His name was rarely in the columns or in trade papers like the *Hollywood Reporter* or *Variety*. If it did, it was usually about him and others involved in some new project or the progress of one already being produced. His reputation with women, so far as she heard, was two failed marriages and rumor of relationships of one kind or another. But as he had both power and money, anything was possible. Anyway, she decided she liked him and liked being in his company, He was always kind and thoughtful towards her. She had heard through the grapevine, however, that he had a heavy thing going with a well-known actress for some time. The story was that he her set up in an apartment in a complex it was said he owned. And one other interesting tidbit of gossip was that the romance was waning.

It was really not her concern as he was obviously not interested in her romantically. And she went on dates, usually to something connected with the industry or a shared meal with a friend. Nothing really serious. Then production started on her show, and she was too busy to think much about those kinds of things.

The series was in its eighth week of filming, and five of the shows had been seen on television. At first, the reviews and ratings had not been as good as hoped for, but they picked up considerably with the third and fourth shows. Everyone connected with it breathed easier now that the ever-present threat of cancellation had passed—for the rest of the season, anyway.

What that meant to Kate in real terms was very good pay plus residual payments when the show was repeated on television, as well as very good money from foreign sales. Marty kept telling her that he was certain to at least double her rate if the show were picked up for another season. He was also, he told her, holding out for a lot more money before he would let her do any magazine covers or posters. What they were offering now was only peanuts. But by next year, they would be begging her with great amounts of cash.

Yes, he told her, things were going to be rosy. And just by the way, he had said, her friendship with Roy Delahunt had not hurt her either. Marty managed to say it without a wink and a nudge, but the meaning was all too clear. She let that pass, knowing Marty well enough to realize that he was not one of nature's most subtle individuals.

Meanwhile, Kate's acting had improved quite a bit, she believed, and she made a strong effort to bring more to her part with every show. Always prepared, diligent about learning her lines, and most important, her timing was excellent; all these made her easy to work with. She was about the only actor on the show who rarely made a mistake and almost never fluffed a line. She was a fast study with a good-to-excellent memory, so she knew her part in the script flawlessly before filming began.

However, she sometimes felt the other actors on the show were not putting out their best efforts, and the directors, too, seemed to require only a certain amount out of them. Still, she wanted to do the best job she could, so she was always well prepared, though she never overreached. Kate always remembered she was there to support the star of the show. She was also very aware of her limits as an actress and the extent of her skills, even though it seemed others were apparently ignorant of the fact that she was a relative novice. But Kate was pretty relaxed about it and no longer belittled her acting talent.

In fact, Kate began to believe she had a real shot at, not stardom, but getting good parts—and soon. She felt more confident with every passing day in the studio. With every scene, she felt the improvement in her competence and performance, which were, astonishing as it seemed, becoming more natural and much easier.

Her voice had become much stronger. Her delivery could be forceful or tender, whatever was required in the script. Her deportment was pretty near perfect. When she walked, she walked with confidence. She certainly knew now how to make an entrance. No, not the hackneyed old tricks. She brought with her, her own presence. All in less than three years. Kate shook her head in wonder. *Wow!* she thought. *Who would have thought it? An actor—a professional actor. A professional actor with a future!*

Kate decided that for the next part, she would dump the blonde wig and go with her natural dark hair. She really felt sure now that she could be a strong performer, and—given the right parts, well, who knows? Kate was excited.

Every now and then, Roy Delahunt stopped by and sat with her for lunch in the studio commissary. A couple times, he had shown up unexpectedly with a couple of hamburgers. She enjoyed that. It was laidback and not interrupted, like when they were in the crowded commissary, and Roy would be greeted or spoken to by several people.

Kate found herself curiously jealous when that happened. She wondered if she were falling for this attractive man. Of course, they were becoming more friendly. Now, more often than not, he kissed her on both cheeks—Hollywood style.

Roy had, after a time, made a perfunctory sexual pass at her which she perfunctory discouraged, with no embarrassment to either of them. It seemed, however, somehow inevitable that they were to become lovers. But just as inevitable was that there was no hurry. They began to see each other for quiet dinners in some out-of-the-mainstream kind of places, not those where the Hollywood crowd or columnists would likely frequent.

Their friendship blossomed in this fashion over several weeks, until Roy, apparently sure the time was right, asked Kate to accompany him to Lake Tahoe, Nevada, for the opening of a new hotel to which he had been invited, along with dozens of screen celebrities of varying levels and a number of studio executives. Kate, perhaps also feeling the time was right, said yes.

Roy Delahunt's seduction of Kate was both unruffled and at the same time, overwhelming. She didn't discourage his initial advances, dispensing with the usual token resistance; they had long passed that stage. By now she knew him well, she thought. And there was no doubt that she was more than just attracted to this charming and worldly man who just happened to be handsome and wealthy.

Kate was ready to fall in love.

From that first night in the hotel suite, their lovemaking was, on her part, receptive and responsive. As for him, he was indeed an expert and a considerate lover, bringing her up from arousal to heights of sexual climatic experience, and then holding her at the pinnacle of that mind-snapping sensation for longer than she could have ever believed possible until she felt she could not stand it a second longer.

Sensing this, he would begin a slow descent, bringing her down gently. And then commence the assent all over again. They missed some of the organized events and one of the dinners in the new hotel that weekend, preferring to eat alone in the suite or snack at the poolside restaurant. They walked around the lake late at night, holding each other tightly. Kate luxuriated in the hot-bloodedness of this new experience. Then they went back to the suite to make love.

Kate had had other boyfriends, of course. Several, in fact. But now that Roy had made love to her, she realized she could hardly call them lovers anymore. Inept fumbling in the back seat of a car, culminating in a quick burst of fire at eighteen, left her wondering immediately afterwards if she were still perhaps a virgin, with a boy she would never date again.

Then there was a college romance of an almost equal insensibility, and a mind-dulling escapade with a solemn professional type, who proved little better in bed. These were her sexual experiences. Other encounters ranged from platonic friendships to warding off boorish hustlers interested in making it with one of the college beauties. So it was only natural that Kate should be overwhelmed by the exciting Roy Delahunt. Never before had anyone taken such possession of her lovely body—or taken her to such a peaks of excitement. She would later come to realize that the sexuality Roy had brought to the surface was essentially in herself. He was the spark that ignited the flame.

Roy had to go to New York City on business, so Kate was left to spend the rest of the long weekend alone before returned to Hollywood to begin working on a new episode for her series. She wanted to go to the airport with him, but he insisted she stay at the hotel, relaxing and getting some sun.

She missed his presence immediately but shook off any slump in the knowledge that she would see him, according to his promised return to Los Angeles, in about four days. She spent that day and a half behind dark glasses at the pool and talked to waiters and others only when necessary, happily daydreaming about the time spent with Roy. Was it love, real love? Yes, no, she had no idea. Vacillating first one way and then the other.

Kate's return to her tiny apartment was, however, disheartening. She made up her mind to move as soon as possible. The next day she called an estate agent who specialized in rentals to find her another place. After seeing several during the next few evenings, she decided on a bright, two-bedroom, bath, and living room apartment on a small block in Los Feliz. It overlooked Hollywood and Vine and the Sunset Strip. Further in the distance, she could see downtown Los Angeles.

It was fairly large and comfortable. She had a small balcony facing west, a reasonably sized pool for residents' use, and underground parking. One of the bedrooms she decided to turn into a kind of den and TV room. It was unfurnished, so she spent the next two weeks in her spare time away from the studio buying pieces appropriate to both the apartment and her personality.

It was against her canny instinct to leave two weeks of paid rent on her old place. But she had a healthy bank account and was earning enough not to worry about scrimping.

Roy was not too happy when she told him about the new place. Since he had never seen it, she wondered why. He told her he thought she might move into a place he had, but she was emphatic on maintaining a place of her own, and he let the matter drop.

They saw each other about one, or at most, two nights a week, usually for an early dinner at a restaurant and then to his house in Beverly Hills, where their lovemaking continued as in Lake Tahoe, unabated and seemingly with no end in sight.

Kate thought about it. Was it love or just sex? Roy had not said, 'I love you.' But then, neither had she.

CHAPTER 10

Roy Delahunt

Roy Delahunt was obsessive about two things. The first he already owned yet was still an obsession. The second was something he wanted and would be harder to obtain, but he was working on it.

During one of her visits to his home, he had taken Kate into his den. At other times, there was a party or some other reason she would be at his house. But this time, it was just the two of them. o

The den was at the far side of the house and wholly separated from the living room, dining room, and all the other wide-ranging areas of the house. In fact, it was in a hallway that visitors and guests really wouldn't it know was there at all. And the door itself did not look like a door in the usual sense of being an entrance. Unless someone looked closely, it just seemed to be part of the wall. The den was a rather small room, more like an elegant sitting room than a traditional man cave. In there he showed her something he prized over everything, or almost everything.

First, he sat her down facing a large, somewhat routine painting of a country scene. A piece of art one might expect to see in a mid-range or even a low-level art gallery. It was on the very center of the wall and seemed to be a permanent fixture. Seated as she was, she could really direct her attention only to what she was facing, the rather uninteresting canvas.

Kate assigned a rather whacky, questioning, expression to her face. Then she looked at him, and in a comic tone, said, 'Sooo?'

'Have patience. You are about to be blown away.' Then he stepped over to a bookshelf. 'Are you ready?'

'For?' She laughed. 'I don't know for what, but yep, I'm ready.'

Roy pulled down a little on one of the books. 'A little dramatic, I'll admit,' he said. 'But it's for security.'

The room lighting dimmed until it was dark. There was a soft buzzing sound, and the painting began to rise and finally disappear into a space somewhere between the wall and the ceiling. The buzzing faded to silence once the painting had vanished. But then the empty wall space was filled by another painting. This one was much smaller than the one it replaced. The painting moved into position, mechanically of course, but the theatricality of the process gave an appearance of the supernatural. And almost as spooky, a sound—one that was so odd Kate could only guess what it was, perhaps a cello or a flute. It was strangely moody but still pleasantly melodic. At the same time, lighting from above and both sides of the painting came on slowly. The lights, too, moved into position so as to illuminate the wall in a quite spectacular fashion.

The lighting coming to life so slowly and the protracted movement of the artwork had Kate riveted now. Then ...

'Wow!'

Kate stared at the piece. After a few moments, she stood and moved to be able to see it from a closer angle. Roy watched as her face came alive. 'Wow, Picasso!'

The subject, or subjects, of the painting seemed to be two youthful figures. Females, no doubt about that. But they were merged in such a way that it was hard to determine where one began and the other ended, and vice versa. It looked like they might be fighting—but maybe not fighting, something else. And there was something else that Kate did not immediately discern. Moving closer, she could see it. The girls' eyes were larger than they might have been—in true Picasso style—and the eyes were those of cats. It was titled *La Felines* and signed by the great painter.

'Well, what do think?' Roy asked her.

Kate didn't answer right off the bat. Instead, she went up to it and moved to look at it from a deeper angle. Then she took a place behind the chair in the center of the room, directly facing the Picasso. After a few moments, she stood back and nodded. Kate was not blown away by the painting, but then again, she was not indifferent to it either.

Kate knew a lot about art from her college days, but she was not so much into nonrepresentational art. Like most people, Kate wanted to know what she was looking at. But she did like it for the great splash of colour, and the subject was bizarrely mesmeric. Then again, it was a Picasso.

'It's different, strange even for Picasso,' Kate replied deliberately. 'I do love the colours, though. They make no sense. Blue and yellow and red, it's all over the place. Yet it works. It's crazy, even mad. Maybe that's what it's about, madness.'

Kate lifted her hands, one on each side of her face, as though she were trying to hold or even grab something, 'It has to mean something. The eyes, I love the eyes. And the colours, weird, crazy, intriguing.'

'Intriguing, eh?'

'You know,' she said, 'I bet everyone who has ever seen it says something different about it. That's what I think is interesting; it means something different to everyone.'

'Hmm.'

'Art teachers say there is there is always something meaningful about every painting. What is it, Roy? Are they fighting or what?'

'I don't care if they're fighting or fucking. It doesn't matter.'

'All right, Roy, then tell me this. What do you think is the most significant thing about this painting?'

'That's easy.'

'Yes?'

'That it's mine.'

⚜

Roy's second obsessions was Harlan Westbrook. Harlan Westbrook was the big man of Hollywood. He could make or break a picture deal in seconds. He could say yes or no, on or off; it was that simple. He was the man. There were others who could do something like that, but Harlan was the only man in Hollywood who could make it a sure thing. Or kill it. If Harlan Westbrook wanted a script to become a picture, he could do in a minute what might take others months, sometimes years, of negotiation.

Roy was obsessed with becoming the new Harlan Westbrook. He had done business with the big man many times over the years, beginning when he first came to Hollywood as a newcomer, getting his feet wet with the lower end of modest productions at first. But those days were long gone. Roy Delahunt had moved on and up. And he never broke the first rule of financing movies: Never put your own money into anything. He used what all the smart men in the business used, the second rule—OPM, other people's money.

Harlan Westbrook was not a nice man. Ill-mannered and arrogant, he was manifestly unforgiving of even the most minor of infractions. He made people pay dearly for any slight or undesirable comment. But there was one good thing about Harlan Westbrook. He looked like what he was—chubby and charmless. Unsurprisingly, he was generally, if not universally, disliked. And there was something else; he was well known for sexually preying on young actresses who came under his purview, in the style of what it was believed of the long-gone boss of MGM, L. B. Mayer, and his famous casting coach. But Harlan was different.

Harlan was demonstrably self-assured about his peccadillos too. He was only too aware that he could get away with pretty much anything. And he did.

The truth was that Harlan wasn't all that interested in the sex. He was more of a wham-bam-thank-you-ma'am kind of lover, except for the thank-you-ma'am part. He was not much of a lover at all. No, it was more about power, it was that he had the power.

It was a fact that some of the actresses, although not finding a coupling with him to be idyllic, in some ways did not suffer from it. It was well known that he had, with almost just the flick of a finger, ended the career of more than one actress who had rejected him. Others, however, had if not exactly thrived had done well.

Case in point—a star, a big star—Gloria Van. It was said she was only at the top because she bedded Harlan on a regular basis. That was true enough. But Gloria was also a tough, mean and shamelessly self-centered. She was a hard-nosed businesswoman, and her business was Gloria Van.

And Gloria didn't have to threaten Harlan to get what she wanted. She had a natural vicious streak that was in no way disguised. Curiously, Harlan was turned on by it, so they both got what they wanted—Gloria her career and Harlan his power-sex. Gloria knew what a sick bastard he was and used it to her advantage. And Harlan, being Harlan, knew what she was doing. In his perverse way of thinking, he admired her for it.

Gloria was universally unpopular with people she worked with and, in turn, had a broad contempt for her fellow actors. She knew that she was not liked, that when people were nice to her, they didn't really mean it. But Gloria didn't care because, in this respect, she had power, power by proxy, but power nevertheless, And they better be nice to her.

There was no doubt about one thing, however, and that was that Gloria Van delivered on screen. She was an all-round top-notch actress. Gloria had gone from being a small-time bit player—a nobody—who, as the Hollywood grapevine had it, Harlan-fucked her way into the big time.

Harlan Westbrook's underlings kowtowed to him fittingly. One thing that encouraged Roy was that Harlan Westbrook never seemed to elevate any of those below him in any of the organizations he controlled to a very high position. A position from which they might start thinking they could one day take over. In fact, he tended to get rid of those he believed might become too ambitious.

But he appeared to tolerate Roy. In fact, during their meetings, Roy sometimes had the feeling that Harlan actually liked him—if it were possible for Harlan to like anyone, a sentiment most people in the industry would seriously doubt.

One of the reasons that caused Roy to feel encouraged was that Harlan had given him his private phone number. That had to mean something. Roy immediately put it on his speed dial but was careful to use it sparingly. More and more, Roy felt that Harlan was positioning him for a move further up the ladder, but Harlan was hard to read.

Yes, Roy wanted to take Harland's place, but one of the outlandish things about the whole business was that he could not do it without Harlan's help, albeit unwitting. It was a question of timing and time. It was time for new blood, and if that meant spilling old blood, that was fine with Roy. But he was not yet strong enough to go to in to all-out war. He would have to bide his time, use Harlan, work with him when he could, and yes, even kowtow if he had to. Then he would be in a position to strike at the perfect moment. Harlan was, after all, the great man, the king. The king Roy Delahunt hoped to dethrone in time. Or it could all come about another way.

There was no doubt in his mind that it was going to happen. And there was one other thing that made any thought of loyalty disappear; deep down, Roy hated Harlan, and taking his place at the top would be a pleasure. In the meantime, he would be patient, bide his time. Anyway, for now one out of two was not bad. Roy still had the Picasso.

CHAPTER 11

The Man from the East

During the last few weeks of shooting for the season, Kate noticed that a number of people connected to the show had become increasingly edgy and less willing to exchange pleasantries with each other. Crabby and ill-humoured would best describe the overall temperament of the crew and cast, and Kate wondered why.

Sure it had been a hard season, with several fourteen-hour days, overruns and reshoots. But in comparing it with the work most people had to do to earn even a modest living, Kate thought this was a breeze, and these people, those actors who were working all the time, were spoiled rotten.

Still, it didn't make her feel too happy that the star and other more featured actors on the show hardly spoke to her, and grumbles took the place of previous greetings. She had outside interests, but she was seeing, for a multitude of reasons, practically nothing of Roy. According to Roy, it was because his already busy schedule had intensified, and he had expanded business interests.

Turning to her work, she tried to fine-tune her performance as much as she could for the last two shows of the series. Rumours abound in a TV studio, not to mention Hollywood itself. Kate heard Roy had bought the controlling interest in the company producing her show. But since she had no way of confirming it, she would have to wait until she saw Roy again.

Not that it mattered much to her personally. If the rumours were true, he would become her boss. But as her ongoing role in the series was hardly primary, it didn't really concern her. Besides, who headed the company at the corporate level was really none of her business.

Another few days passed without any word from Roy, and Kate's efforts to contact him were thwarted at his home and office, the housekeeper and secretary both saying that he was unavailable or out of town. Kate began to reason that no one need be that busy, and if Roy wanted, he could see her or at least return her calls. *Has he gotten tired of me?* she wondered. All kinds of thoughts enter her mind as she lay awake in the lonely apartment. *Is he seeing someone else?* Of course, it had to be that. She hated him. She loved him.

When his business quieted down, he would be back to continue their love affair. Maybe he wouldn't. He could have any girl in Hollywood, in the world! But she thought, as her heart pounded thunderously, hardly being contained in her chest, *Do I love him? Does he love me? Yes he does. Maybe not. I don't know. He never said he did, but then neither did I. I would know, wouldn't I? Oh, shit, shit, shit! I can't think of this anymore. Shit.'*

Following this pattern for several days and nights made her nervous and miserable. More miserable than she thought it possible to be. Thank God the last show of the season was about to start.

Then surprisingly, Roy called her cell. Thrilled and happy to hear his voice, she forgot the unhappy past three weeks at once. He was sorry, he said, that he wasn't able to spend time with her, but he was sure she understood. Of course she told him she did.

'How about tonight?' he asked.

Tonight's fine.'

'Okay,' he said. 'I have a business friend in from the east who may join us for dinner, okay?'

'Yes, sure. Of course, fine, whatever.'

'I'll send the car for you around seven, okay?'

'Sounds good.'

'Then I'll see you at the restaurant Scandia.'

'Roy I—'

'Okay. See you then.'

'Oh, Roy, I really need to see you, Roy and …'

Kate was still talking when she realized that he had placed his hand over the speaker and was speaking to someone else. *Maybe it's someone in the office,* she thought. Then Roy turned to her again. 'See you then. I'll send the car.'

He cut the connection.

Kate slowly replaced the phone in her pocket and leaned against the wall, not knowing whether she felt happy or dejected or both at the same time. Or if that were even possible. Happy that after such a long separation she would see him again and unhappy because they would not be alone.

She wondered again how much she was in love with him. Was there a way to figure that out? All she could think of now was that she would see him. But where was this love for this man leading her? And she wanted to be with him and in his bed more than anything. She fantasized about the sexual pleasure they would share from the first minute they were alone. Oh, God, she needed to be with him.

Kate saw the sleek black limousine pull up in front of her building and ran quickly down to meet the driver, who was now on his way to ring the buzzer to her apartment. 'Good evening, miss.' the elderly, well-mannered driver said as he opened the door for her.

'Good evening. Thank you.' Kate was surprised to see there was someone sitting in the car's rear seat as she got in. But it was not Roy. 'Oh, hello,' she said as she took her seat.

The car was not one of those stretch jobs, nothing like it. It was just a full-size luxury car. But it did have the usual trappings associated with the word 'limousine.' She heard a soft voice from the far side of the rear seat. 'Good evening, Kate.'

'Oh, good evening, Mr …', Kate offered politely.

'Monty.'

'Monty? Mr Monty?'

'No, call me Monty. Monty's fine.'

'Is Roy at Scandia?'

'Don't know, maybe. Said he might be late. He's pretty busy right now.'

The car moved smoothly through the evening traffic on Sunset Boulevard, and Kate took a look at this man from the East. He was about forty or so, she figured. In the intermittent flashes of the lights from the street, she could make out his features and physique fairly well. A layer of fat covered what was basically a sizeable frame. He had a puffy, well-fed face that disappeared into a large head. Not such a good-looking man, Kate thought, but not really ugly, either. He could be quite-good looking if he were in better shape.

They made small talk about aspects of California lifestyles, and Monty asked her a little about herself until they reached the restaurant. She was disappointed to find that Roy was not there. They followed the maître d', who met them at the entrance, making their way to the booth Roy had apparently reserved.

'A very large, very dry Beefeater martini,' Monty told the man before he could get away. 'What will you have?'

'Nothing right now. Oh, wait. Yes, a glass of white wine, please.'

The man thanked them and passed the order on to the waiter, who had appeared with little bread rolls and celery sticks.

'Now, tell me more about yourself,' Monty said. 'Roy told me some, but I'll say this, you're certainly a looker.'

'Thank you. Well, I finished college in the Midwest and came out here. Just finishing my second season of a show. Have you seen it, by the way?'

'I think so. Maybe.'

Obviously a lie, Kate thought.

'Don't get a whole lot of time for that kind of thing.' Then he sort of just sat there gawking at her. Like this guy had never seen a pretty girl before.

Kate thought perhaps she should say something, so she told him a little more about the show, concluding quickly, 'That's about it, really. Do you think Roy will be long?'

'Don't worry,' Monty said, patting her hand. 'Ah, the booze.' The waiter placed the drinks on the table, and Monty quickly grabbed at the long-stemmed glass. 'Here's to you,' he said, taking an enthusiastic gulp of the powerful drink, leaving just a little floating around in the bottom of the glass, less than enough to keep the olive wet. 'Silver bullets, we call 'em back east. Hmm, and this is a good one. Waiter, another.'

He moved his finger in a circular motion. *That must mean a silver bullet in the east,* Kate thought as she observed this young-old man demolish two more in quick succession, while she took only sips of her wine.

Kate became more and more anxious as they waited for Roy to arrive. And Monty became, with the effects of alcohol coupled with a pompous manner, more and more forceful. Leaning over her in the booth, his hand made a grab at her leg. She avoided it adroitly and asked politely to be excused for a moment.

Away from the table, Kate headed to the rear of the restaurant, where the restrooms were located. With a shaky hand, she dialed Roy's phone number on her cell phone, hoping that he would answer. Kate counted each buzzing sound to eliminate all the mad thoughts racing through her mind while squeezing her eyes tightly shut in an effort to have him answer.

Hello, there,' Roy's affable voice came to her.

'Oh, Roy. Thank God!'

'How's it going? Having a good time?'

'Roy, why aren't you here?'

'Yeah, well I got hung up. How's it going?'

'You mean with this asshole?'

'Come on, he's not that bad.'

'Oh, yes he is. He tried grabbing my leg under the table.'

'Well, you do have great legs.'

'Be serious. He's getting pretty drunk and pretty obnoxious.'

'Yeah.' Roy laughed. 'I'm afraid he's not too much of a drinker. He really can't handle it.'

'You can say that again.'

'Look, Kate, so he's getting a little drunk. Just go along with it.'

'How long before you get here?'

'Not for a while.'

'Roy, I believe this friend of yours thinks he can get me into bed. Doesn't that bother you?'

There was silence from the other end.

'Roy!'

'I'm here.'

'Does it bother you?'

'What?'

'This clown thinks he's going to get me into bed!'

'I can hear. You don't have to shout.' Roy's voice softened, 'Look, it's only a one-time thing. And besides—'

She cut him off. 'Are you kidding?'

'No, I'm not kidding,' he said, his voice becoming harder. 'This is a money guy and could be important to me. Don't be such a hick. Don't you understand?'

Kate felt a sickness in her stomach and a chilling fear at the same time. Could this marvelous man whom she had loved with such a passion, to whom she had given every emotion in her being, could this man she admired, could he be asking her to sleep with this awful jerk?

'Roy, are you saying you want me to sleep with him?'

'Look, all I'm saying is be sensible. He's an important money guy. That's all.'

'And I'm not important?'

'Oh, you know I didn't say that. Of course you're important.'

Tears welled in her eyes. The sickness started to become a numbness. The fear became a non-feeling.

'Are we finished, Roy? Are you finished with me?'

'No, of course not.' He paused for a long moment and then added, 'Not necessarily.'

So that was it. Sleep with this jerk or lose Roy.

'Are you still there?'

'Yes', she answered calmly. 'I'm here.'

'Look, Kate, I'll come over to the studio tomorrow. We can have lunch, just you and me. Okay?'

'Okay', she answered. The spirit to fight was gone from her voice.

'That's my girl,' he said in a voice that seemed to say, 'Come on, cheer up. Worse things can happen.'

'Your girl?' she asked with more than a trace of scorn.

'Come on, Kate. Hey, let's make that dinner tomorrow night, just you and me.'

She didn't answer.

'Kate, okay?'

'Yes, Roy.'

'Fine, Kate, fine. Now you have a good time, you hear?'

'Yeah, sure', she mumbled. 'A good time.'

'There you go. Bye.'

The phone lay dead in her hand.

How long she stood there staring at her phone she had no idea, but a light tapping on her shoulder brought her back to reality. Another girl wanted to use the wash basin Kate was standing in front of. Kate wiped her eyes and hurried past, making her way back to the booth, and Monty.

When she returned to the table, she found Monty in slurred conversation with the occupants of the adjoining booth. Then, turning to her, 'Well, you sure took your time', adding in a lower voice and arched eyebrows, 'Everything all right?' He laughed out loud at his unfunny quip.

Kate sat in a kind of stupor, seeing him but not really paying any attention to him as he talked on. 'Waiter, some drinks here. Hey, did you call Roy?'

The question startled Kate a little. 'Yes.'

Monty chuckled. 'Yeah, he said you would.'

So the whole thing had been orchestrated, a set-up.

He moved closer to her and put his hand right in the center of her crotch. She didn't move or say anything.

'Hey, why don't we just skip dinner. 'Let's go back to my hotel.'

'Really?' she asked.

'Really!'

Kate stared at him. Straight into that puffy, drink-reddened face, realizing now that he was rubbing her through the light material of her dress.

She suddenly came to life. She stood up and picked up her pocketbook from the table. He began to rise, but she stopped him by placing one hand lightly on his shoulder. The other hand she drew back all the way behind her head. Had he not been so drunk or his reflexes a little better, he might have been able to avoid the solid, open-handed wallop that Kate delivered flush on the side of his face with a booming *wham!* It was a mighty slap heard around the restaurant. Heads turned in their direction.

Having never hit anyone in her life, Kate had no idea she would be so effective. But that she had been was evidenced by the absolutely stunned look on Monty's pudgy face and the ugly red welt taking shape from the corner of his eye all the way down to the corner of his mouth.

'Fucking bitch!' he bellowed in sputtering disbelief.

The waiter rushed up. 'Is everything all right?'

'Oh, yes,' she answered. 'Just bring him another silver bullet.'

Kate favoured the waiter with a charming, sweet smile. She turned and walked out at a dignified pace to the applause of those at nearby tables.

CHAPTER 12

La Felin
(The Cat)

Kate waited contemplatively in the den, thinking carefully about what she planned to do. The housekeeper had been hesitant to let her in at first, but Kate was able to act her way in and wondered if this woman ever slept.

Roy would be surprised to see her there, no doubt about that. Well, that was not the only surprise he would get. She looked over at the Picasso and wondered if it was really the original Roy had said it was. The thought lasted less than a moment. Kate decided that it was unquestionably the real thing and that it must be worth a fortune.

It hadn't been hard to find the book that activated the mechanism. One gentle pull, and it came down smoothly, just the way it had when Roy showned it to her. It was all connected. The first light faded and was replaced by the softer spotlights centering on the painting.

She picked up a notepad and wrote in large letters the script. *Let's call it a script,* she thought. When finished, she ripped the page from the pad and placed it on the table.

A telephone with several buttons sat on the table beside the chair. Kate noted the right button; it was number 1 on the speed dial. From the other side of the house, she heard the front door open and close noisily. Roy was home.

She could hear his voice saying something to the housekeeper, loudly and angrily. No doubt she had immediately encountered him at the entrance of the hallway to inform him of the guest waiting for him. Kate moved to stand close to the painting, taking a glass jar with her, and waited.

He is on his way now, she thought. She stood stock-still, took a couple breaths, and composed herself.

He walked in quickly and stood at the door, an indignant look on his face. 'What the hell are you doing in here?'

'Come in, Roy,' she said calmly, waving him to the chair in the middle of the room.

'Who the hell do you think you are', he yelled, 'barging in here uninvited? And what the hell is my painting doing there? How the hell did you get it down?' He turned from the painting and faced her. 'You've got some nerve.'

'Sit down, Roy. Sit down and shut up,' Kate said slowly. She was still calm, but there was a menace in her voice.

'For Christ's sakes, what the hell do you think you're doing?'

'Take a look at the note on the table, Roy.'

He scanned the writing quickly. 'What the hell is this?'

'Now pick up the phone, put it on speaker, and press number 1 on the speed dial.'

'Like hell I will!'

Kate lifted the opennecked glass jar she held and moved closer to the painting. She smiled sweetly. 'Acid, Roy.'

'What?'

'Sulphuric acid, Roy, instantly destructive.' Speaking slowly and very calmly, she continued, 'Pick up the phone and press the button and read that to the man who answers. Now!'

'You kidding. That's probably just water. Where the hell would you get acid?'

'Car battery.'

'I don't believe it.'

'Press the button. Now!'

Kate went up to the painting and held the glass jar in closer. Then she took up a throwing stance.

'Wait!' He held up his hand in a stop motion and thought about it for a second. 'I still say it's water.'

'Maybe you're right. Feel like taking a chance?'

He laughed but it was not sincere, and she knew it.

'Listen, Kate, I—'

'No! You listen.' There was real menace in her voice now. 'You have a ten count, or it's bye-bye, Pablo!'

'You're crazy.'

'Nine', Kate barked.

'It's water. I know it's water, you crazy bitch!'

'Eight, seven.'

Roy shook his head. He smiled but let his hand hover over the button on the phone.

'Press number 1, and put it on speaker,' she yelled at him vehemently. 'Now!'

He hesitated.

Kate lifted the glass higher, closer to the painting. 'Six!'

He didn't move.

Kate's arm started forward. 'Five! Four!' Kate moved into a total throwing stance and yelled, 'Three!'

He moved his hand closer to the button but still did not press it.

'Two!' she screamed.

'All right, all right.' He pressed speaker on the phone and then the number one button. Almost immediately, a voice on the other end came back loud and clear. 'Harlan Westbrook.'

Roy spoke quickly, an apology already in his tone. 'Harlan, I'm I, I—' That's as far as he got.

'Read it! *Now!*' Kate went into a genuine throwing motion. One quick move, and the painting would be destroyed.

75

'Listen to me.' Roy began to read what Kate had written, speaking very fast and very loud. 'Listen, you, you ignorant turd!'

'Who the hell is—'

'Roy Delahunt, and I'm telling you that you can shove your company up your ass and go fuck yourself!'

'Hang up,' Kate told him quickly.

He pushed the off button and slumped down in the chair as though he were a dead man, and in a way he was. And he knew it.

Kate moved away from the painting and closer to his chair. She looked down at him and shook her head. 'You always told me to trust my first instincts. Roy, you should have trusted yours.' Kate lifted the jar to her lips and took a sip of the water. She Looked at his pale face for a moment and then walked slowly out of the room, down the long hallway, and out of the house.

CHAPTER 13

Viva Mexico

Kate endured a miserable night of emotional torture. And the next day at the studio was not a whole lot better. Of course, she had to concentrate on the job, but every now and again, she started thinking about the night before, and that would make her angry all over again. She wavered between hating Roy and hopeful that he might call. He didn't. And she was angry with herself. Could she have handled things differently? Of course she could have. Then again, she thought, *No way!*

Kate normally did not let anger of even of the slightest degree get the better of her. It was not part of her nature. But during breaks, her mind was in something of a jumble because of anger. First because of what had been done to her, and second was directed at herself for being such a fool. The angers seemed to alternate and sometimes overlap each other.

At first, she thought she had no idea how she was going to make it through the next two days to the end of the show for the season. But she did. Kate was determined that she would never just walk through her part, so she worked harder. She did more than just make the effort. And it was worth it. She turned in one of her best performances, and she knew it. It was confirmed by the episode's director with strong and positive remarks to her later. She was happy with that because he was more of a striver for excellence than the other two directors, who sometimes seemed to sleep through the job.

Kate thanked her lucky stars that her part was a respectable piece this time, much better than usual. She had a lot more to do, and given her state of mind, was grateful for it.

As customary for the last episode of the season, the show focused hard on the star while dropping in a few clues about the next season. But Kate had made her presence felt. Of that there was no doubt.

She had also made up her mind about what she would do after it wrapped. Kate did not feign sickness to avoid going to the traditional wrap party. She thought about doing that but decided to go instead. She had a couple of drinks, talked to others of the cast and crew, thanked those she had to thank, and got away quickly.

Once at home, she packed a bag and caught a plane to Acapulco the next day.

Kate stayed in Mexico for several days, checking into at an excellent hotel that had pretty much everything she could possibly want. The only person she told was her agent, Marty, texting him where she could be reached.

She mostly kept to her room when not on the beach or at the pool. She quickly discouraged the hits put on her by beach Casanovas. Kate told the pool and cabana boys she didn't want to be disturbed, adding a good tip to make sure they would pass on this information.

As well as sunning, reading, resting, and sleeping, Kate passed the time straightening out her mind, thereby ridding herself of the spectre of Roy Delahunt. Perhaps she would never be completely rid of him, she thought when the distress was at its peak. But self-discipline and her inherent sense of reality gradually rescued her from any deep distress. Not really surprising herself, she began to feel better, appreciating just being and being alone.

Towards the end of her stay in Mexico, Kate called Marty at his office. He was friendly and cheerful and seemed pleased to hear from her. He never touched on the fact that she belted some big shot.

But she suspected that he knew about it. She told him she would be returning soon but didn't want to do any work at all until the show started again. Marty said that would be fine. She asked him about the new contract, and he told her contracts were never sent out until the show was officially picked up by the network. He would let her know. He didn't mention Roy Delahunt. Nor did she.

Kate left Mexico for Hollywood soon after that, feeling much better. Her innate common sense had been her real salvation. Sure, she had been through a rough time emotionally, and it had drained her physically. But Kate counted her blessings. She had saved nearly all her net earnings and had very healthy bank and savings accounts. And she had a good job to come back to after the hiatus.

But still there nagging at her was the love she had felt for Roy, the betrayal, and a thousand other things. But those distressing bouts that occurred from time to time were quickly becoming less frequent. Her will to deal with them became stronger with each passing day. Nothing of a permanent nature had really happened to her. So she had fallen madly in love with someone who was not right for her. Roy had played her and groomed her. There was now no doubt in her mind that Roy Delahunt had groomed her, groomed her! Anger would well up for a moment when she thought about it. So she would rid her mind of the thought straightaway. It was over, and she knew it was over.

Love was like a sickness, love-sickness. Even if it wasn't real, genuine love, it was still a sickness, Kate reasoned. She had been sick, and now she was well. The patient had cured herself. It was over! And time would completely eliminate him from her memory.

Men, she also told herself at the time, were anathema to her. But she knew she would get over that feeling too. She was far too young and sensible and with a healthy outlook on sex not to realize that. But not for a while, a little of the pain was still there but fading fast.

Kate spent only two days in Hollywood before setting out for Minnesota by car, stopping wherever she wanted to enjoy a leisurely pace and the freedom it gave her to just go as she pleased. It took a few days to reach Circle Pines. The quiet and tranquility of the summer brought Kate pleasure. She was happy in the familiar surroundings of her former, less-complicated days. Real people in a real place.

But there was a tiny nagging. She realized that she was anxious to get back to work. Kate was not lazy; she liked to work and work hard. The work ethic was strongly based in her family and community backgrounds.

She phoned Marty from time to time to inquire about her contract. But there was no news. This did not concern her too much. By now, she knew the industry's inertia when it came time to deal with down-the-line series' characters.

The time she spent in the Midwest brought Kate a peace of mind so strong she knew it would sustain her as long as she lived. The thing with Roy Delahunt was nothing more than an adventure that she had to go through, she now reasoned, to steel herself against adversity. She needed to stop thinking with her emotions and use her brain. The patient, she decided, had fully recovered. And her diagnosis was right.

Kate made a fast return trip to Hollywood, arriving at the apartment just three days after saying goodbye to Minnesota. After a good night's sleep, she called Marty's office. A recorded voice gave her a referral number. As she dialed, she kept thinking the number sounded familiar.

'Titan Studios.'

'Oh, sorry. I think I've dialed the wrong number. No, wait. Is Marty Steinman there?'

'One moment please. Extension 719, putting you through.'

Kate thought that sounded familiar, too, as she heard the connection clicking through.

'Mr Steinman's office.'

'May I speak to him?'

'Who's calling?'

'Kate. Er, Catherine St. Clair.'

'One moment, please.'

Kate waited for what seemed a long time before she heard Marty's voice on the other end of the line. 'Hey, Kate, how are you?'

'Fine, Marty. What's happening? You have an office at the studio?'

'Did you get my letter?'

'No.'

'Okay. Well, see, I closed the agency.'

'No, really?'

'Yeah. It's all in the letter. I guess you'll get it.'

'I still don't understand. You mean you're not my agent anymore?'

'That's right.'

'Just like that?'

'Well, yeah. I guess I'd had it too many years. Anyway, that's it.'

'What about my contract with the show?' she asked, a little desperation creeping into her voice.

'Oh, that's all in the letter. Maybe I can get you a copy of it.'

'Yes, okay,' she said. 'But what about it?'

'It wasn't renewed.'

'What?'

'Yeah. They wanted to change the format somewhat, and sorry, they dropped you.'

'But they took an option.'

'That's right, but it wasn't picked up. You know.'

'No, I don't know! Marty, I have to see you.'

'That wouldn't do any good. You see, I'm no longer your agent.'

'Can you just do that?'

'Oh, yes. All legal, notarized, and, well, that's the way it goes. That's showbiz, babe.'

'Don't babe me. I don't think you can just—'

'Listen', Marty's voice rose in volume as he interrupted, 'now get this into your head. The agency is closed, I'm not your agent anymore, and your contract wasn't renewed. The end. Get it?'

'No, I don't get it,' Kate shouted into the phone. 'You can't just—'

'Look, I don't have time to listen to you gripe.' He hung up the phone.

Kate was stunned but thinking fast. She dialed the number again.

'Titan Studios.'

'This is Enid Johnson', Kate said, 'over at the Writer's Guild. We need some information regarding the executive line-up at Segway Film and Television. Can you give it to me?'

'I'll give you personnel. Hold, please.'

'Thank you.'

Kate asked the same question of the person who answered at personnel and was given the names of directors, producers, executive secretaries, and accountants. Two familiar names came over the phone to her.

'Martin Steinman, executive in charge of production, and the company Segway is owned by Roy Delahunt and Associates. Was that the information you require?'

'Yes. Thank you.'

'You're welcome. Thank you for calling.'

At that very instant, Kate knew for a certainty that her acting career was as dead as a cemetery; her destruction was complete. It would be useless to call other agents or producers as the word would be out. She had committed the unforgivable. *Yes, I really learned a lot during the years to improve my acting ability, but not enough to get to the top.* She had nothing to offer that a thousand—no, a hundred thousand girls—didn't have.

Roy had to do it, she reasoned, to appease the odious Monty. Even if he didn't want to, he probably would have done it anyway to get her out of his hair. After all, she could become an embarrassment. Well now, it was really over.

Then there was the thing with the 'acid' that she had pulled. That alone would be enough to get her kicked off the show. And she figured he would probably have to do a lot of ass-kissing if he was ever able to get back on Harlan Westbrook's good side.

Over the next few days, Kate terminated the lease on the apartment. And apart from the few things she wanted to keep, sold all her furnishings to some man the building superintendent brought around. Then she got into her car and headed east. She was going to New York City and would never return.

She had committed the unthinkable, the unforgivable. Not what happened with Roy; that was personal, and he would get over that. And she was sure that over time, he would be able to mend fences with Harlan Westbrook because, in the final analysis, they needed each other. No, it was the thing with the guy from the east. Monty.

Slapping Monty was the real transgression. Kate had committed the unforgivable, the most egregious of all Hollywood crime. She had offended the money.

CHAPTER 14

Zero Minus Forty-Three Hours

'Shit!' Luke reacted with a start to a shrill buzz that came from the measuring device attached to the first truck. It wasn't all that loud but, in the confines of a narrow iron and steel conduit, the sound was strident and to Luke, jarring. The buzzing noise ran away on up the tunnel and came echoing back to them.

They had been pushing through the cavernous water tunnel and at the sound of the signal, Steve called for a halt to check the device. He made some calculations on a small pad and carefully noted the time.

They were moving single file, each hauling one of the carts that were not unlike an old-fashioned wagon but bigger and much sturdier. With four wheels and a handle, and being constructed, as they were, of the best material machined to the highest standard, made them well within the hauling abilities of all of the men. Even the tiny Luke was able to pull his truck without too much of a strain.

Steve stopped the hike as soon as the buzzing began, and he and Mark bent down to inspect the dial on the device. While they were thus engaged, Luke walked back to Matt at the rear.

'I guess I'm a little uptight down here. Doesn't it bother you?'

'Luke, that's only natural, first time and all. I'm used to being underground one way or another. You'll get used to it.'

'Shit, I don't want to get used to it!'

'Okay, but it will happen anyway.' Matt smiled. 'Don't worry about it, Luke.'

'Hell of a buzz,' Johnny said. 'Hard to miss that.'

'Yeah, it's the warning that we're near the spot we want,' Steve explained, studying the device. 'Not too much further now. We'll get two more buzzer warnings. Okay, we can start moving it again now, Mark.'

Mark pulled on the lead truck, and the others followed.

They resumed going forward again, on through the seemingly never-ending tunnel which only a short time before had been a vast, rushing watercourse. They moved slower this time however, and more cautiously, apprehensively perhaps waiting for the next buzzing sound from the measurer.

Then it sounded. Not as loud, it seemed, the second time, perhaps because this time they were expecting it and Steve was quicker to turn it off.

'Just a matter of feet now,' he said, in a voice that he hoped would have a calming effect on the others. He knew how aware they were of what the slightest miscalculation would mean to all of them.

Again he and Mark carefully checked the device against his book, the electronic pad and watch. When satisfied that they were on schedule and the measurements were correct, he told Mark to pull the truck forward once more.

They moved more cautiously now. Each step carefully placed in front of the last with the full knowledge that the slightest inaccuracy would place them beyond any chance of getting out of the tunnel alive.

The third and final buzzing came with both relief and uneasiness. Mark stopped the truck instantly. He pressed down hard on a lever that sent out two metal bars, locking the wheels of the little truck into immobility, automatically disengaging the buzzer.

Steve walked a few feet ahead, and with one simple movement, set up a small table complete with a battery lamp. So light and portable was it, that this workbench seemed almost like a magician's trick when it appeared and was about the size of a thin briefcase. Then he and Mark laid out the plan book, pad, and other small pieces of gauging equipment on it. Together they leaned over the little table, making certain calculations and consulting various instruments, charts of the underground tunnels, and the plan book. Meanwhile, Johnny and the others began unloading some of the gear from the trucks.

'Agreed?' Steve finally asked Mark.

'Yes, agreed.'

'Good', Steve said. 'Now check it all again.'

Mark hesitated for the briefest of moments and then bent over the table once more. The next ten minutes were tense and disturbing for the others as they watched him going over the figures and computations again, while Steve checked his other instruments. He was more careful than compulsive about it, assuring himself that if anything were to go wrong, it would have to be something beyond his control. And certainly not any miscalculation of timing.

Finally, Mark straightened up and moved away from the table. 'That's it.'

The other four waited quietly as Steve looked for a few moments, first at the wall and then even longer at Mark. 'Be sure, Mark,' he said quietly. 'We only have one shot at this.'

Behind the wall would be either what the calculations told them was there or disaster. There would be no going back and no way forward.

Mark thought for a few seconds before answering. 'Absolutely,' he replied quietly.

Steve nodded but didn't give the order to go ahead for almost a full minute. Then, 'Okay. Go ahead, Mark.'

Mark drew on the wall with a sort of chalk material that glowed in the semi-light. He created a four-sided diagram, exactly two-and-a-half feet square, measuring carefully as he went.

Steve turned to the others. They looked a little nervous, no doubt about that, but he decided each of them was holding up well. 'Bring your gear up, Johnny. We go in here.'

The gas bottles were the largest and least portable of their equipment. They lay torpedo fashion along the specially built truck. Getting the trucks past each other proved too difficult, so each of them had to be moved up several yards to make the adjustment.

Whether this was part of the plan or not, Steve never said. But if not, then perhaps a few precious minutes were lost. Quickly, however, Johnny was in position, and as soon as Mark handed out welders' goggles to the others, Johnny lit the oxyacetylene torch which ignited quickly with a loud splutter.

He fine-tuned the flame until there was a blue aura surrounding a tiny white point. Sparks flew off the wet steel wall as the cutting flame bit in. But the sparks soon splattered away, and the torch moved smoothly, piloted by Johnny's expert hand. The square cut was almost completed when Johnny paused to allow Matt and Mark to attached two suction holding devices to the plate that was soon to be removed.

The last part of the cutting was accomplished, and the plate fell heavily into the hands of the two men holding the suction grips. Matt and Mark placed it down carefully several feet from the wall. Steve came forward to find that behind the steel was a wall of old red bricks. Steve nodded to Matt, who after rolling up his sleeves, began smashing into the bricks with a sledgehammer.

A hole was quickly made. And with each crunching blow struck by the robust Matt, it became bigger and bigger, until it was large enough for Steve to call a halt so that he could put his head through. With the aid of a flashlight, he was able to see what was behind the brick wall. After a quick glance, he stood back and motioned for Matt to continue.

Soon the hole was sufficiently large enough that they could go through. Steve first and then Matt, who according to the plan, sat down immediately to rest while Luke joined Steve.

The others passed all the equipment through the hole, and last, they carefully maneuvered through the cut-out portion of the steel wall, that was still held by the suction grips. When all the gear had been placed on the other side, Mark and Johnny went on through.

In the glow of two truck headlights placed opposite each other and slightly turned to face the aperture, the area began to take shape.

This was created as a tunnel, but with rough and unfinished walls, more like a man-made cave, when the water tubes were laid long ago.

Mark removed the suction holders and placed them on the reverse side of the cut-out steel plate. When Johnny was ready, Mark and Matt held it in place, and Johnny began to weld it back into the wall of the tunnel. He spot-welded in several places so that Matt and Mark could let go. And once the plate was self-supporting, they removed the suction grips.

The welding continued smoothly, but it was still a tediously slow process because Johnny had to be sure of completely sealing the aperture.

'He's in the station now,' Steve said, checking his watch. 'It's now five forty-five.' He paused for a moment, calculating in his head. 'In fourteen minutes, twenty-eight, no, twenty-six seconds, he's going to release two thousand tons of water per minute into that tunnel.'

The welding showed one whole side had yet to be completed as Johnny moved into position to start the final leg, beginning at the bottom of the crack and working upwards.

'What if it's not finished by the time the water reaches it?' Luke asked Matt in an anxious whisper.

'It has to be finished,' Matt murmured back.

The welding was going painfully slow, and sweat began to trickle down Johnny's face. And time was moving faster than the welding torch.

'We should get the hell back,' Luke said, an edgy tremble in a voice that he didn't recognize as his own.

'It wouldn't help,' Mark said grimly. 'Anywhere down here will be fatal if it's not finished.'

Steve checked his watch and then looked back to the welding line. There was still way too much to go. He shook his head, turned to the others, and thought about waving them back. *For what*, he wondered. No one moved anyway, perhaps to indicate trust in their partner.

'Oh, shit!' Johnny snapped, twisting his mouth from side to side. 'Not now!'

'What is it?' Steve asked.

A feeling of imminent disaster ran through all the men.

'What the hell is it, Johnny?' Steve asked again.

Johnny didn't take eyes away from what he was doing. Both his hands were as steady as rocks as he moved the torch along, little by little. Again he twisted his mouth.

Steve looked at him closely. 'What is it?'

'Nothing.' Then, 'Shit, shit. Sheeeit!'

'What the hell is it?' Steve asked yet again.

'Itchy nose.'

'What!'

'My nose is itchy. Scratch it for me, will you?'

'Somebody scratch his nose,' Steve ordered.

'Not me!' Mark said.'

Luke scrambled up to Johnny. 'I will!' He almost shouted, perhaps thinking that they could all die because of an itchy nose. He reached in careful not to bump the torch and scratched Johnny's nose the best he could. After a moment, Johnny told him that was enough, and Luke moved away.

'For the want of a nail, the horseshoe was lost,' Matt whispered. 'For the want of a horse, the king was lost, and for the want of a king, the battle was lost.' He looked at Luke. 'It's always the littler things.'

'The little things, yeah.'

'Good job, Luke.'

'How much longer, Johnny?' Steve asked the sweating welder.

'Five or six minutes.' There was no waver in his voice or in the fine join he was making with the torch.

'No, Johnny. Three minutes!' called Steve.

Luke said quietly to Matt, leaning in close to him. 'It's nearly done, man. Only that bit along one side.'

'That's true, it is nearly finished,' Matt said. 'But see, Luke, any crack in it would tear off the whole plate, and this place would fill in no time. It must be completely sealed.'

'It will be closed,' Steve said, an edgy rebuke in his voice.

All eyes strained toward the thin welding line Johnny was making.

Steve checked his watch. Thirty-four seconds to 6 a.m.

There were still several inches unsealed and gaped ominously. 'Couple more minutes,' Johnny said under his breath.

Mr Tubbs stood waiting at his command post, watching as the seconds ticked off on his old, giant pocket watch. He double-checked the even older clock on the wall above his head.

'Stand by!' he shouted.

Seconds ticked by until the clock on the wall registered six o'clock. Mr Tubbs straightened his back, filled his lungs, and bellowed, 'Open the gates!'

The men in the station who had been waiting for the order, swung into action, pulling switches and turning wheels.

Deep underground, huge steel gates began to open, immediately releasing a huge body of water into the tunnel, crashing and tumbling faster and faster. As volume increased, speed increased as the gates opened to their full width. Thousands of tons of raging water raced towards Johnny and the others.

◈────────◈═══◈═══◈────────◈

I'll be the first to go, was perhaps the thought running through Johnny's mind. *The plate will take me out.* But his hand never wavered, and the line of welding remained perfectly straight.

Then they began to hear it. At first, the sound was a dull moan, but within seconds, the sound became louder, ever increasing until it became a deafening and terrifying roar like a tornado, and the ground beneath their feet began to shake violently.

'Stand back!' Johnny called. But the thunderous noise coming towards them was so loud that no one could hear him. He knew it, but he shouted urgently, 'Get the hell back!'

Not even for a millisecond did Johnny let his eyes move from the welding.

They heard him yell this time, but nobody moved.

It was too late for that anyway.

Steve put his hand on Johnny's shoulder. 'Steady, Johnny,' he said, leaning in close. 'You're almost there!'

But the water had arrived.

Suddenly, a tremendous jet of water gushed from the unfinished part of the seam. It hit Johnny in the chest with a great force, knocking him backwards, and sent the welding torch flying from his grip.

'Holy shit!' Luke shouted, but no one could hear him.

Johnny clambered back into a position near the jet stream. And after retrieving the torch, he went back to work, trying to seal the gap through the blast of water.

It appeared to those watching as though Johnny was moving in slow motion, but the jet was becoming, although still intense, smaller and smaller. And in what seemed a very long time, the jet began to subside, and the last of the seal was done. The steel plate was back in place.

Johnny turned off the flame and slumped in a heap right beside the weld, exhausted. He felt around his chest to see if any ribs had been broken. They were not, but he could feel fierce pain from where the blast of water had hit him in the chest.

Steve moved over to him. 'Good job,' he said quietly. The relief in his voice was all too evident. Johnny looked at him as though for the first time. After a moment, he nodded.

Luke breathed a loud, 'Wow!'

Matt called, 'Well done, Johnny!'

There were a few moments when nobody said anything. Finally, Steve called in a loud, clear voice, 'Rest. We rest.'

The roaring water could still be heard, but it was less now that the initial torrent had settled to a steady flow.

'Now we rest,' Steve said again while consulting—although he didn't need to do so—the plan book. 'We have a forty-five-minute rest period.'

'Okay by me,' Johnny said softly. The pain in his chest was already beginning to subside.

'Luke,' Steve said, 'break out the food and drink rations.'

'You bet. But if it's all the same to you, I'll take my rest period a little further away from that,' he said, pointing to the recently sealed hole. 'How about you, Matt?'

'No, Luke!' Steve told him forcefully. 'We rest here, have something to eat and drink, and then move on. The whole operation is timed down to the second. Any deviation cannot be permitted.'

'Right, yeah, of course. Sorry.'

They took up various positions. Luke handed out the prepacked rations, and they began the rest period.

Steve checked his watch. 'We're on time, precisely on time. A little extra rest. That's good.'

Luke wanted to say something. 'I learned something today, Matt.'

'What's that, Luke?'

'Nose-scratching.'

'We learn something every day.'

'Some things, I guess.'

'Everything.'

'Okay. What's the best lesson you ever learned?'

'That's easy.'

'Yeah?'

'Did you ever hear anyone say, "I had no option"?'

'Sure.'

'Well, they were wrong.'

'But sometimes there is no option.'

'Wrong, Luke. The lesson—there is always another way.'

'You mean in …'

'In everything, there's always another way.'

'I'm not so sure about that.'

'Trust me, Luke, there is always another way.'

'Okay, if you say so.'

'I do.'

They were quiet again for a few minutes.

'Shit! You know something?' Luke asked as he settled himself in another position. 'We almost got killed. Right, Johnny?'

Johnny didn't answer. But Mark did: 'That's life.'

'Ah, yes. Life.' Matt declared, 'Life—the thing that will often play a joke on those who take it too seriously.'

'I'll tell you something else,' Luke went on. 'When you think about it, no one would ever know we were down here. I never really thought about that till now.'

Steve didn't want this kind of talk to continue. 'Everything is going as planned. We are on time. Just stay cool.'

Luke nodded. 'Yeah, cool,' he answered, but hardly confidently. 'Cool, huh?'

'Staying cool is not always that easy when things change,' Mark observed. 'And when they do, that's when you have to have

93

circumstantial flexibility. You have to deal with a change of events, you know. You have to deal with the circumstances.'

'Men don't rule circumstances,' Matt said. 'Circumstances rule men.'

Mark raised his eyebrows questioningly and looked at Matt. 'Herodotus,' he said.

'Ahhh, yes.' Mark nodded. 'Herodotus.'

Nobody said anything for a few moments.

'Man,' Johnny said, wiping the sweat from his face and neck. 'I could sure use a beer.'

'Okay, let's see,' Mark replied earnestly. 'What would you say to a Heineken?'

'Maybe. No, how about the Mexican one. Ah—'

'Dos Equis?'

'Ummm.'

'Corona?'

'That's the one. Yeah, cold.'

'Of course.'

'I mean ice-cold.'

'You got it,' Mark said, fake rummaging in one of the duffle bags. 'You want it with a lime slice sticking out of the bottle's neck?'

'Now you're talking.'

Luke looked over to Matt. 'We have beer?'

Matt smiled his no.

Another silence. Then Luke took a deep breath and let it out with a loud sigh. 'Like I said before, what the hell are we doing down here anyway?'

Johnny shrugged. Then almost under his breath, he replied, 'Maybe it's just for laughs.'

Luke harrumphed. 'What laughs?'

Johnny leaned all the way back against the wall, closed his eyes, and thought about it. Then he grinned, perhaps remembering some other time. 'There's gotta be a few laughs.'

CHAPTER 15

A Few Laughs

There was no better welder anywhere than Johnny. He could work for any outfit he wanted, construction or demolition. No doubt he was a master of his craft. He earned good money and never saved a dime.

Johnny was also, in a manner of speaking, a ladies' man. Very attractive to the ladies, in a restaurant or bar, he always caught their eyes. Here was a man who was not handsome, not in the way most people think of handsome. He was rough-looking, in fact. And no one could call him a great dresser as he wore mostly jeans and a heavy shirt in winter and a tee in summer. Yet Johnny could have almost any woman. But Johnny was picky. He liked good looks, of course, but more important was good company. He himself was great company, a jokester who liked to laugh.

His general demeanor was casual indifference, yet attracted the attention of women of all types, ages, and financial statuses. Just your average working man with what some would call animal magnetism; he was catnip to the ladies. Forty years old, easy-going, and one could say generally insouciant, and the girls still fell over themselves to get to him. Johnny not so much. He liked the ladies, but anything that smacked of a permanent nature, and he was out of there. Any talk of settling down was not for him; a house and talk of kids were not his things. He was happy the way it was in the small apartment he had shared for years with Mush.

Mush was different, not big, not robust, not handsome. Mush was what you might say on the other side of handsome, with a long nose, hardly any chin, and small rat-like eyes. Mush admitted that he was, 'no oil painting'. So what? And since no woman in her right mind would willingly go to bed with him, by hanging around with Johnny, he was able to score from time to time with one of Johnny's girlfriend's friends.

Johnny had plenty of people he could call friends, including workmates and guys he had known or kicked around with for years. But there was nobody like Mush.

Mush was always coming up with something, a hustle of some kind to make easy money. But none of his schemes ever worked out. He wasn't a bad guy. In fact, he was a good guy, just unlike Johnny, who worked hard and liked to work hard. And Mush was, in his odd way, smart, although he would never have admitted it. He needed someone to look out for him, and that someone was Johnny.

And he made Johnny laugh. Mush was funny; he knew he was funny. He didn't have to try to be funny, he just was funny. The way he spoke, the way he told a story—he would sometimes act it out. Mush was just a naturally funny guy.

Born and raised in the same Brooklyn neighborhood, Johnny and Mush were as different as it was possible to be. Johnny was good=looking in the rugged way; Mush was not in any way. Johnny was big and strong, Mush small, scrawny, and ugly. And Johnny was his best friend.

Over the years, they had pulled a lot of shit together and raised a lot of hell just for laughs. A lot of it just happened other things, while others were at Mush's instigation. He would say, 'Hey, Johnny, let's go do so and so'', and Johnny would say, 'Are you nuts? I'm not going to do that shit.' And they would do it. Johnny would shake his head and say that he was the one who was nuts.

To tell the truth, Johnny went out with some ladies over the years because she had a girlfriend Mush could get together with. And that was never easy because Mush was about as good-looking as a truckload of elbows. Mush described himself as 'unique'.

Johnny had this 'from time to time' lady friend who lived on Broadway, close to the top end, near Central Park. Eleanor was a nice lady. And Eleanor was wealthy. Well, she had to be wealthy. She lived in a beautiful apartment on Broadway which she owned. Eleanor had met Johnny at a bar one night and invited him over to have a drink at her place. That was a couple years ago, and Johnny was a 'now and again' visitor. Mush occasionally tagged along, usually heading for the kitchen when he got there. Mush liked to eat—a lot.

Even though Eleanor was a rich socialite and a lady through and through, she was not a snob. She liked the down-to-earth Johnny. His freaky sidekick, not so much. She would look at Mush and do an inside-her-head shudder. But he was Johnny's friend, so that made it, if not okay, at least unobjectionable. Anyway, Mush was funny in an odd sort of way, and most important, he was Johnny's friend, and Johnny was her friend.

Of course, the congenial Eleanor had many suiters—suiters of the moneyed class. But she found most of them to be stiff, stuffy, and pompous in their utter correctness, affected or real. Eleanor, ever gracious, made sure she didn't show it, but they bored her to death. They were no fun. For fun, there was Johnny.

And Johnny liked her. It was a casual thing with no hooks either way. Johnny didn't care that she had money; he had no interest in that kind of thing. No, it was not her money. It was more like having someone way above his social status who he could be friends with and have a few laughs. And they laughed a lot every time he went to her apartment, jokes and pranks.

Both Johnny and Mush were pretty good cooks when it came to lower-end fare, nothing fancy. They would bring over all the fixings and put together a humungous pot of Irish stew or spaghetti or rigatoni or sausages and onions or something. And with that commonplace food and several beers all round, Eleanor always had a great time. Eleanor invited Johnny over many more times than he came. She really liked him.

Sometimes she thought there could a possibility that Johnny might move in with her. Or because she had money, even something more serious. But after she got to know him well, she knew for sure that was not Johnny's style.

For Eleanor, it was a way to let her hair down, so to speak. She could, for an afternoon or evening, forget for a while that she was a well-respected society lady with lots of money and the obligations that went with it. She was generous to a fault and involved in many charities. That meant committees and such that took up much of her time.

None of that that mattered to Johnny. He never thought of her as anything but a nice lady, someone he could have some fun with without ties of any kind.

Eleanor was a trifle overweight but not in the least zaftig. If she were to lose maybe five or six pounds, she would be close to perfect; she already had a great shape. She was around forty, give or take, very good-looking with blonde hair and an exotically beautiful face. Eleanor was divorced and sexy.

And about the sex. She enjoyed the freedom it gave her. And she was good at it.

There was this one time that she invited Johnny to her apartment to watch the Macy's Thanksgiving Day parade from her third-floor windows. They enjoyed a nice meal that she had thoughtfully prepared. And when Eleanor and Johnny were finished, they began talking about nothing in particular, just regular chit-chat.

'That was a real feast, Eleanor. You're a great cook.'

'Thank you, Johnny. I'll tell you what is great, and that's to see someone who really enjoys food. It makes it all worthwhile. And you're really not a big eater; you just enjoy good food.'

'Uh huh.'

'But don't talk about Mush here. He's a champion eater!'

'Huh?' Mush said, absently lifting his eyes from the table for a second and then back to the food.

Johnny started to say something but then stopped. Eleanor noticed. 'You were going to say something, Johnny?'

'Oh, nothing. I was, no nothing.'

'Go on.'

'Well, okay. What I was just going to say, well, you should have seen my brother. Now he was an eater!'

'You have a brother?'

'Twin brother.'

'Really? Johnny, you never said you have a brother, and a twin at that.'

'It's not something I talk much about.'

'Identical twins?'

'Couldn't tell one from the other.'

'Wow', she said. 'And he ...'

'Disappeared.'

'What?'

'Yeah. He ran away twenty years ago, and I never saw him again.'

'Did you try to find him?'

'Looked all over.'

'Oh, Johnny, that's terrible. I'm so sorry.'

'Yeah, well, there you go. What you going to do? That's how it goes.'

'So sad,' she said, taking his hand.

'I'd sure love to see him again,' Johnny said, shaking his head. 'But that ain't going to happen.'

'What was, I mean is, what is his name?'

'Oh, ah, Clyde. Yeah, Clyde.'

'Clyde. Oh sweetie, that's so sad.'

'Yeah, well.'

'Isn't that sad, Mush?'

'Huh? What?' Mush answered vaguely. 'I wasn't listening.' Mush got to his feet and took some of the dishes to the kitchen.

Eleanor glanced at the antique clock on the mantelpiece. 'Oh, it's time. Hurry up. The parade's going to be here in a minute!'

She moved quickly to one of the wide windows to look down at the parade. It was just about to roll down Broadway, right under Eleanor's third-floor window. The great Thanksgiving parade. There was no place in New York with a better better view of it. And she was not going to miss any part of it. 'Hurry up boys, it's here!' Eleanor settled herself and leaned out the window to see the parade pass by.

With Eleanor's attention directed to the street below, Johnny dashed silently out of the apartment door. He raced down the three flights of stairs to the entrance hall and out of the building, whizzingpast the uniformed doorman and onto the sidewalk.

Meanwhile, Mush came back into the living room. Eleanor called to Johnny over her shoulder, 'Come on, sweetie. The parade's coming down Broadway right now. Hurry, get on over here!'

Mush looked around the empty room, shrugged, and took a position beside her at the window. The way her apartment windows were angled, she could only feel his presence, not see that it was Mush, not Johnny, cosying up beside her.

Johnny ran about half a block up Broadway, turned, and joined in, marching along on the outside of a championship high school band that was belting out, in true brass band fashion, a really hot, swing version of 'The Lady Is a Tramp.'

Seconds later, the band passed right under Eleanor's window. He had a broad smile on his face that seemed to say, 'Hey there!' Johnny began waving.

She saw him right away, but not really *him*, just some guy in the crowd. But as Johnny's waving became more insistent, she *really* saw him. A full-sized smile broke out on her face. And she waved back. Then it hit her!

Her eyes widened, and her mouth opened with a full-blown shriek. Then it *really* dawned on her. 'Oh my God, it's … it's … it's Clyde. It's Clyde!'

She grabbed onto the arm beside her but kept her eyes on the figure marching down Broadway. 'Johnny', she screamed, 'it's Clyde, it's Clyde!'

Eleanor kept yelling while frantically shaking the arm beside her—until she turned her head into Mush's 'unique' face. She let out another shriek, one almost as loud as the hullabaloo from the street.

Johnny returned to the apartment to fing Eleanor standing in the entrance, shaking her head. 'Really, Johnny. I mean, Johnny and Clyde. Who in the world would fall for that?'

'Ah, you.'

'Like a ton of bricks, you rat.'

She took him in her arms and kissed him on both cheeks. She smiled because deep down, Eleanor knew that he didn't do it to her. He did it for her.

No doubt Eleanor had a healthy sense of humor. It was always easy to make her laugh, even if the joke was on her. 'Oh, Johnny', she said softly as she held him close, 'you do make me laugh.'

They later reminisced about that Thanksgiving. About that and other good times they shared.

But now Mush was gone.

He had driven off with two neighborhood yahoos when Johnny was pulling an all-night welding job in Jersey. They had crashed the car, and Mush died in the hospital the next day, Johnny at his bedside.

Eleanor cried inconsolably when Johnny told her what happened to little Mush.

Johnny didn't go to Eleanor's place after that. He figured that as long as he was hanging around, she would never find the guy she should really be looking for. She was a good person and deserved someone who would be there, not just for a few laughs, but for her always. And who would make her happy.

CHAPTER 16

Zero Minus Thirty-Eight Hours

Apart from the physical energy they had expended, there was an emotional drain. Steve was not surprised as they had come close to being killed. They needed time to settle down a bit. So they rested. Even though they knew it was according to the plan, and they were all still strong, they welcomed the time out.

What made them strong as a group was, perhaps, that they were all quite different in character as well as separated by age, knowledge, and experience. If they were the same or even similar, they would have the same feelings and fears.

Luke asked why the cut-out plate had not burst in on them as they thought it could. 'It sure looked like it was going to.'

Mark said it was because of the fine old steel the tube was made from. But Steve said Johnny's expert welding was what held it together, and the plate would have torn off under the force of the water had he not almost completed the seal. As it was, the tiny unfinished potion had almost been catastrophic.

'Go over and take a look,' Steve suggested. 'That seal he made is absolutely perfect, and that's what did it.'

Mark did just that. He went over and closely inspected the seal. 'Yes, it's perfect, all right. That's what held it, no doubt about it.'

But Johnny shook his head.

'It's both. Without that great old steel, I couldn't have done it. It was remarkable that the metal was still in such great shape after the pounding it must have taken all those years. We were lucky.'

Luke shuffled around, trying to find a comfortable spot. But he was unable to and gave up. Instead, he eased himself down on the rough tunnel floor and leaned back against one of the little trucks near, where Matt was doing pretty much the same. 'I guess the door is really closed on us now, huh?' he said to the old man quietly sitting there.

'I don't think of it that way, Luke.'

'Well, there's a lot of water between us and the outside.'

'Yes, a lot,' answered Matt.

'And there's no of going back, is there?'

'That's true, there's no way of going back. But we're not going back. Luke, in all the great things in life, it is important not to have any way to retreat.'

'No retreat?'

'The explorer Roald Amundsen was on his way to the North Pole in 1912 when he told his men that. It is important that we have no retreat.'

'Well, I guess that's us.'

'No retreat means we can only go forward.'

Luke took a long look at the old man and then started eating the packaged food before speaking again.

'Like I said before, I guess you're used to this, Matt.'

Matt thought for a minute and then nodded. 'I suppose.'

'I mean, like this, you know, underground.'

'No.'

'But you ...'

'Maybe miners say they get used to it, and I said you would get used to it, didn't I?'

'Yep, that's what you said.'

'Well the truth is most people would never get used to it.'

'That me.'

No one said anything for a few minutes. Mark reopened the topic as he moved over to squat near them. 'Rough down there,' he said. 'I mean in the mines.'

Matt nodded. 'Sure, but they're up to it. Miners are tough men.'

'Dangerous, too, huh?' Luke commented.

'Sometimes.'

'You have any close calls, you know, like this one?' asked Luke.

Matt looked at him for a long minute and then nodded. 'Well, yes. One.'

'What was it?'

'An explosion.'

'Were you down in a mine?'

'Yes.'

'What happened?'

'Not now, Luke,' replied Matt. 'Another time, perhaps.'

Luke pressed the man. 'Let's hear it, Matt. I mean, this is the perfect setting for a story like that. Anyone else want to hear about it?'

Mark shrugged. 'Why not?'

Matt looked over to Steve, questioningly. Steve looked thoughtful but said nothing and apparently had no objection.

'The old Glenburn mine', Matt began, 'a cave-in. Cave-ins happen from time to time in the shafts, but this was a big one. 'Matt took a long look at the area they were in right now. 'Maybe this is not such a good idea.' It seemed as though he wasn't going to say anything else, but at the end of a long sigh, he continued. 'An explosion in another shaft nearer the surface, above where we were. We didn't know it then, but five men were killed in the initial blast. But we sure felt it, though. Shook the hell out of the whole mine and caused a cave-in. For me and the gang I was with, it blocked any way to get out. They would have to dig us out from above. There were eight of us, and we were stuck. We knew right away that we were stuck.'

The others listened more closely now.

'The thing about being in that kind of situation is mostly air. You are going to run out of air pretty quick. And there were a lot of us—eight—in a small area, so we were going to use up the air fast. Four of the guys were hurt by the falling rocks; one was badly hurt.'

'Were you hurt?' Luke wanted to know.

'Just a scratch. I was okay.'

'Sorry, go on.'

'Well, after the explosion—we knew what it was, of course—we could move around a bit, looking for a way out, even though we pretty much knew there wouldn't be one. But you know, we had to be sure. So we looked for where there might be pockets of air. No luck. We were between the coal face in front of us, and behind us, the drift that was well and truly blocked solid by all the cave-in debris. We knew that they would have to come get us if we were ever to get out. We would just have to wait for them to get to us.'

Mark looked at Matt and then up the tunnel beyond the dim light. They were now in darkness. Steve was listening, but at the same time, he was checking his notebook.

Matt went on. 'As it happened, we had enough air. Not like fresh or anything like it, but it was air. Anyway, we had to take care of the injured the best we could, which wasn't much. Then one of them died. He was right under a huge part of the roof that fell in on him. It crushed his chest, and he was bleeding badly. He died the first day. There was nothing we could do to save him. I was the senior man and was only sent in with this gang to do a regular check. It my first day with these guys, so I didn't know any of them too well. I didn't know him at all. He was the worst hurt. And he died.'

Someone coughed.

'The three others who were hurt were not too bad. They'd be okay if we ever got out of there.'

Nobody said anything. Matt went on.

'Well, we knew they would be trying to get to us as fast as they could. We could hear the drilling and the noise of the machinery getting louder, closer all the time. One guy swore he could hear voices; they were that close, he reckoned. But it was just being down there. The mind can play tricks on you in a situation like that. This guy swore he could hear voices, even at times identifying workmates. "Can you hear him? That's old Tom," he shouted. "Good old Tom."

'The others just shook their heads, thinking maybe they would all start hearing things that weren't there. Days passed; actually, days and nights were all one to us. Hope started to fade.'

They were riveted now. No one stirred as Matt told the story that he had, by this time, become more immersed than he had wanted. He paused for a minute to look around the group in what gloomy light there was. What he could see of their expressions told him that he shouldn't have started this damned story. He even wondered if he should stop. But one of them, he wasn't sure who it was, said a barely audible voice, 'Go on.'

So he did.

'There was this one guy, only a boy really. I didn't think he was hurt that bad. Well, after a time, it looked like he wasn't going to make it. You had to figure maybe none of us would make it. But there was a strange feeling that seemed to, I don't know, like infect all of us. It seemed like if anyone should make it, it should be him. Maybe it was because he was the youngest, just a kid. Even though no one said anything, the feeling was that he had to make it out, and that kind of kept the rest of them going. It was like that was the mission, to save this kid.'

No one said anything. Matt went on as though not talking to anyone at all. He seemed to be looking at nothing. Perhaps he was looking inward.

'But the boy got worse. He could have died at any moment. But their will, they willed him to stay alive.'

It seemed that Matt, by vague gestures, could actually visualize the boy as if he was right there. He looked down again, deep into his memory. 'One of them, an older guy, leaned in close to him and said, "Hold on, boy. Only a little longer."'

Matt's voice faded to a feeble whisper. 'Hold on boy.'

Only the dull hum of the water passing through the tube offset the otherwise complete silence that surrounded them. No one moved. Matt shook his head, took a deep breath, and decided to bring the story to an end right there.

'They got us out on the ninth day.'

They waited for him to continue, even though it was clear that Matt would say no more.

Steve broke the silence. 'Time to move.'

They got to their feet and began moving along the tunnel.

This part of the journey was much rougher going, and the little trucks were hard to negotiate over the rocky pathways. Even so, they made steady progress. They occasionally came across some long-abandoned work area, complete with discarded machinery, iron ties, and tracks.

The ceiling came down to meet them at times. Johnny and Steve, the tallest, had to stoop to protect their heads from the stony 'roof' where they were. Other times, they encounter large cave-like places with underground streams, some of which were fast-flowing, unknown to most inhabitants of the great city overhead. There was no light coming from anywhere other than the battery-powered lamps on the carts.

'They're not much, but I'm sure glad that we've got these cart lights,' Luke said to Matt, who was just in front of him. 'Without them, it is just blackness. And it's scary down here in the dark.'

'The dark is nothing to be afraid of, Luke,' Matt counseled. 'Some people are afraid in broad daylight.'

'I suppose so, but I can hardly see anything.'

'Hmm, would that man could see a little clearer, or judge less harshly those he cannot see', he shook his head, 'not understood.'

'Not understood?'

Luke could not really see Matt through the diffused light of the carts. All he could make out was the outline of those great broad shoulders.

They didn't say anything for a while. Then, 'Matt?'

'Yes.'

'Did the boy get out?'

Matt took a long time to answer. Then he stopped and turned. Even in the dim light Luke could see a melancholy expression on the old man's face that seemed to belie his answer.

'Yes, Luke, he got out.'

'Ahh', Luke murmured pensively. 'Good.'

Matt turned and started the little cart moving again. 'All right, then,' he said more keenly. 'Let's get on with it.'

CHAPTER 17

Zero Minus Twenty-Nine Hours

Most of the time, there were compensating rises and falls in the shaft so that they had remained on about the same level. But then the path began to take a slight downward slope, taking them deeper.

They arrived at a waterway. It was narrow, and the water was deep. And even though the little river was not really moving very fast, it was moving. On the other side of the water was a ledge about five feet higher than the level they were on. They could see another tunnel leading off that one.

While Luke, Matt, and Mark unloaded the trucks, Johnny and Steve securely lashed a small cannon-like gun between two large boulders near the edge of the river. The gun's barrel that was a little more than eighteen inches long, with a bore of half an inch. Johnny loaded it with a harpoon made of fine steel with ribs along both sides. Once loaded, the harpoon protruded from the barrel by about a foot. A long, coiled nylon rope was then attached to the harpoon.

Once in place, Johnny aimed it at the wall on the other side, a few feet above the ledge. Steve nodded, and Johnny pulled on the trigger lanyard. There was a deafening roar, and the harpoon with the rope attached sped across the water and buried itself deep into the rock face on the other side.

The barrel was reloaded with another harpoon. Johnny changed the direction of the gun and quickly dispatched the harpoon into the wall, about six feet from and roughly the same height as the first harpoon. To make sure that the harpoons were securely driven deep into the wall, Johnny pulled on each rope with all his might, trying to dislodge them. The harpoons held fast.

Satisfied, he and Steve attached a canvas bosin's chair to the nylon ropes. 'Check it again, Johnny.'

'Okay.' Johnny pulled on the ropes again with the same result, making doubly sure that the rig would sustain the weight of a man going across the fast running water.

Steve nodded. 'That's good.'

Steve sat in the chair. Johnny fastened him in securely by tying off the Kevlar straps around his chest.

The others took their positions, ready to haul on the ropes. After taking a careful look around him, Steve motioned with a nod that said he was ready. Johnny checked that everyone was in place, and Steve slipped over the edge.

He went down close to the water. Matt and Mark pulled with an even strain on the tackle, and Steve began to cross above the swift current, smoothly and quickly.

Once on the other side, Steve got out of the harness, and the chair was pulled back to the other side.

The next to cross was the tiny Luke. Being so light, he made the trip in half the time Steve took. Steve helped him out of the chair harness, and sent it back across the water to the other side.

Johnny removed the chair from the hooks. He replaced it with a large canvas bag. They transported all the equipment to the other side in four trips. Then it was time to say goodbye to the little trucks that had served them so well.

From now on, they would carry the remainder of their gear, which was by that time much depleted. The gas bottles and torches were left behind at the water tube. And the food packs and water bottles had all been discarded after use. The harpoon gun and the emplacements were also left behind. What they would need from now on were the lightest and the most portable.

By the time all the gear had been sent over, as well as Johnny and Mark, it only remained for Matt to make the passage. He strapped himself into the chair quickly and signaled for the others to pull on the nylon ropes.

'Hold onto your britches, Matt. I'll get you over in no time,' Luke called.

'I'll take more than you alone, Luke, for this fat old man,' Matt called back.

The others took up the ropes. Johnny called, 'Ready, Matt?'

'Haul away!'

Matt was much heavier that the rest of them, and he knew it as let himself gingerly over the edge. He went down faster than any of the others, and his feet barely stayed above the fast-flowing waterway. But then the ropes began to sway back and forth with an uneven motion and became more difficult to control. Even so, it all seemed to be going well and as planned.

Johnny and Luke hauled, and Mark got in front of Luke to lend a hand. Then Steve did the same, hauling on the rope behind Johnny.

'All right,' Steve called out. 'Take a more even strain that will stop the swaying. All together now, pull!'

Matt was getting close now. Luke leaned over the edge, ready to help Matt onto the ledge when he got just a little closer.

Steve felt a jolt on the line and turned to see that one of the harpoons had begun to lose its grip in the rock wall. Small chunks of rock were falling from around the spike.

Mark yelled. 'Hurry! Get him now. The spike's coming out!'

Steve turned to see the other spike was now coming lose. With each sway of the chair, the even more crumbling rocks fell from the wall.

Matt's legs dipped into the water up to his knees. Then suddenly, he started to go lower and lower with each pull of the rope. The swaying increased dangerously. That and the water current began to pull him away from them. Each pull seemed to set up a counteracting swinging motion set up by Matt's weight, and the steel bullet was slipping further out of its socket.

As they pulled harder, Steve could see they were beginning to win the battle. The gap between Matt and those on the ledge began to close. Matt was almost there.

He reached up to grab the ledge. At the same time, Luke leaned over as far as he could to grip the old man's hand as soon as he could.

He was there! Luke's hand touched the outstretched fingers of Matt's desperate grasp. 'Just an inch or two more, and I've got him!' Luke shouted. 'Come on, Matt!' The two hands touched again for a second. But just as they did, Matt swung away again.

Steve moved over to Luke. He knew Luke would never be able to haul Matt up and onto the ledge without help. Matt was coming closer again.

With one more great haul by the other two, Matt was suddenly within reach. But then the steel spike came completely out of the wall. The rope went slack, and Matt was pulled away. His head sank into the swirling water. And he disappeared.

Utter dismay appeared on Luke's face as he shouted wildly, 'Matt! Matt!' Luke jumped up and started to unzip his overalls.

Steve shouted at him, 'Stay where you are!'

'But, Matt!'

The others frantically took up the slack of the rope. So far, the second bolt was still holding fast. But of Matt, there was no sign.

Luke stared at the place where Matt had gone under. He hollered at Steve, 'We have to get him out. We have to—'

'Keep hauling on the rope!' Steve interrupted. 'Pull, pull!'

At that moment, the other spike flew out of the wall. And the rope that it was holding went slack. Not even a second passed before Steve grabbed the rope and lowered himself over the edge.

'Tie off both lines together. Wait till I tug on it, and then haul like hell!' he shouted. Then Steve started swimming furiously with the current, quickly reaching a rocky bend in the river. Then he disappeared from their sight.

<hr />

Kate woke with a start. An unsettling feeling ran through her whole body. The thought that something had gone wrong gripped her. The sensation lasted for long moments, until she was completely awake and able to drive the thought from her mind and let her body relax.

How had all this started anyway? She couldn't remember exactly. It wasn't the night Steve left her apartment after that mess with the phony car accident. *No,* Kate thought, *it was before that.*

Maybe it started for her when she first met him. *Bang!* Just like that! Perhaps it was fate that she should even meet him at all. Was it fate that brought them together? *Yes,* she thought, *it had to be fate. Or maybe it was karma.*

What was karma anyway? Was karma the same as fate, predestination? No, she decided, not karma; karma was different. Then Kate began thinking about something else, the thing he told her about the sun or the stars.

She lay there luxuriating in the comfort of the huge, old, four-poster bed and remembered how he told her about the origin of the plan. It was on a trip they made to the Grand Canyon. Kate thought about how they stayed up all night, waiting for the dawn to come. Lying there, blanketed up together on the balcony of the tiny cabin that overlooked the great chasm. Steve next to her, not only in the warmth of the covering and his body, but the warmth of his gentleness and his strength all at the same time. And then the thrill of it all when the sun's rise wondrously tiptoed over the north rim with the first rays of a new day. And how, in moments, the whole world came alive.

That was when Steve told her about the old lady and his plan. She was not stunned. Not dumbfounded. Not astonished. Those thoughts did occur to her, but only later, when she realized she probably should have been at least surprised, even astounded. But she wasn't. And the fact that she had not been reinforced her judgement that what he said had to have right behind it. Indeed, the way he had explained it to her, well, it did have a measure of right. There was absolutely no doubt that Kate was not the type of person who would follow blindly. She was too much her own person to do that. And there was something else. Kate had her own reasons.

It all seemed so long ago. But of course it wasn't. And the cold reality that it was actually happening made her shiver a little if she dwelled on it. So she made up her mind not to think about it at all.

Instead, she thought of what her life had been like before she met Steve. Life before Steve. And as far as that went, he had seemed completely incurious and asked her no questions. He told her that no one should feel obliged to explain to anyone, especially to a friend.

Steve never asked about her life before they met. He just accepted what she told him. He didn't ask, not because he wasn't interested, but if she wanted him to know about anything, he felt she would tell him. If not, then it didn't really matter. Naturally, she told him everything over the course of time. So they talked about everything; there were no secrets, lives—loves—achievements—disappointments. And there was a bonus.

One of the things they talked about was her abhorrence to the massive amount of damaging facial make-up that was palmed off on girls from an early age. And about her idea, when she could figure it all out, to produce a make-up that was made of entirely natural and harmless ingredients. Maybe even a small company. Who knows? But as she told him, she hadn't figured it all out yet. Kate wore no make-up. With perfect skin and features, she didn't need it.

Of course, during her time on television, she had to be made up. But she had insisted that the amount of make-up should be only what was absolutely necessary.

Kate recalled that long, spectacular, Grand Canyon night he told her how everything had fallen into place for his plan. 'You see', he had said, 'it's like an eclipse of the sun or a unique alignment of stars. All the elements are in the right position for this one slice of time, and those elements may never be the same again.' Events that could only happen with all those elements in place. At times, she thought, her life had been like that. So she understood.

She remembered also thinking of him in curious ways. He was the most vibrant man she had ever met. And without question, the most unwavering. Her thoughts strayed again.

He was down there now. The man she cared for so much was in danger. Something could go wrong, and she would never see him again. Kate put the thought from her mind right away. She loved him, and he loved her. And the bonus? He was her friend.

Maybe it was karma after all.

⁂

'Let's just start pulling,' Luke yelled.

'No,' Mark yelled back at him. 'Wait for the signal!'

Minutes passed as they waited anxiously, but there was no tug on the line.

They had arranged themselves for the best leverage possible on the narrow ledge, ready to operate as a team as soon as they got the signal. But there was nothing to tell them that Steve was alive at the other end of the rope. They looked at the bend where the river flowed, but there was nothing.

Suddenly, a strong tug!

With every ounce of their combined strength, they pulled on the nylon rope. The slack rope slowly became taut. And then straight and tight as a steel rod. A hand appeared out of the murky water, quickly followed by the old man's white hair. Then Matt's head burst to the surface, sputtering and coughing. With Steve right behind him.

He had found Matt clinging to an outcrop. Steve had quickly wound the rope around Matt's chest and under his arms. The old

115

man was in bad shape, but along with Steve, pulled tenaciously on the nylon lifeline. Between those on the ledge hauling, Matt's indomitable determination, and Steve's strength, they closed the gap separating them.

Gradually, they dragged him closer, until they had a firm grip on his coveralls—then an arm—and then up. It took all of them to haul him out of the water and finally onto the ledge. Then it was Steve's turn, which was accomplished quickly.

Matt was soaked, shaken up, and completely exhausted. But the good thing was that he was otherwise uninjured. They got the wet coveralls off him; Steve was able to do the same thing without any help. Mark collected clothes from one of the duffle bags. He took out the outfit they were to wear at the very end, and Matt and Steve put them on. They looked incredibly nonsensical in their present surroundings. Later, when what they had been wearing were dry enough, they put them back on.

Luke fixed all of them something to eat from the food packs.

Once dry and rested, Matt insisted that he was perfectly all right. Steve formulated a new distribution of packs and bags to be carried the rest of the way so that the old man strapped on one of the lightest backpacks. The extra weight was shared equally among the rest of them. Steve then had Matt walk in the middle of the line, behind he and Johnny, and in front of Luke. Mark brought up the rear.

Before they moved off, Matt said, 'Thank you, Steve.'

Steve nodded. 'Anytime.'

'I don't know how you did it, but I believe I owe you all a pretty big thank you.'

'Oh, shucks.' Luke grinned., 'It weren't nothin'.'

'Quite amazing, really,' Matt went on. 'I mean, you being on this ledge the way you were gave you practically no leverage, really no good place to stand. And even with Steve pushing me through the water, well, it was quite a feat.'

'Nope,' Mark the engineer, disagreed. 'With Steve's help, you saved yourself.'

'I don't think—'

Mark interrupted. 'If it hadn't been for your strength in pulling yourself back, we could never have gotten you to the ledge. It was a combination—us and you. But mostly you and Steve. Trying to pull a dead weight through water that was running, even slowly, would be impossible.'

'Well, I guess—'

'And you had to be exceptionally strong to do it.'

'Mark's right,' Luke agreed. 'You two had the strength. We just helped.'

'And that's not just ordinary strength, either,' Johnny chipped in.

Matt smiled and quoted, 'Nothing gives you more strength than dire necessity.'

'Oh?' Steve said, looking at Matt.

'Euripides.'

'Wow', Luke said, 'you know a lot of that stuff. Don't you, Matt?'

'Yep, I do like books.'

'Television and movies for me.'

'Oh, I like them too. But there's something about books. You see, books don't tell you everything. And by not telling you everything, well, that lets your imagination kick in, and that's a good thing. Keeps what's in your noddle ticking over.'

'A lot of books, huh?'

'Some, I would say, only some. If you want, Luke, I'll give you a book that does have a lot of stuff in it. Things that were said a couple millennia ago can sometimes give us direction, or point us in the right direction.'

'I think I'd like that. Thanks, Matt.'

Then, one after the other, they disappeared from the ledge and through yet another, though smaller tunnel on their way to rob a nice old lady.

CHAPTER 18

Martha Brady

Martha Brady did not come from a high-born family, or from money for that matter. The Brady family, like many others, would be considered unapologetically lower-middle class. Her father owned a mixed grocery and grain business on the Totenham Court Road, that he ran with the help of two assistants and a counter clerk. He had no wife; Mrs. Brady had succumbed to a flu epidemic that had swept through London some years before, when Martha was only seven. Therefore, as well as attending a nearby grammar school, Martha had been obliged to help out in the store before and after school since a very young age.

Martha didn't much like serving customers at the counter of the store. She was happiest working in the office. As she grew older, and because of a natural forceful character, Martha gradually took over the entire running of the business.

The management of money, anything to do with the bookkeeping—the adding and subtracting of lengthy columns of figures—suited her well, and she proved to have a knack for it. Moreover, her father was a canny businessman, and Martha had always been one to watch and listen.

No, Martha was not from money or from high-born connections, but she assumed the statuses of both, from then on and forevermore, the moment vows were exchanged on the seventh day of May in the year 1853 at St Martins in the Fields Church between her and Herbert Westerbury Montague. She became a lady of utmost propriety in every respect and resolutely maintained that position for the rest of her life. For as it was said in those days, Martha had married up.

Her young man was employed at a nearby bank and had become a regular customer of the grocery store only because he was smitten with the girl he first spied in the small office at the rear of the shop and occasionally on the other side of the counter. From the time of their first meeting and over the years, he became increasingly captivated by the lovely Martha.

But time was of the essence. Wealthy, good-looking, and refined Herbert would be leaving England soon. So he preceded boldly, proposing marriage by way of her father, the custom of the day, and was accepted. So Herbert and Martha were wed. The young—he twenty-six years old and Martha barely twenty—newly married couple left England one week after the ceremony on the good ship *Wayfarer*, bound for the new world where Herbert had inherited a small bank in Boston.

Even in progressive America, it would be considered unseemly for a lady of quality to be involved in business. It would be considered quite inappropriate for a woman to be engaged in any way with commerce of any kind. It was just not done. Curiously, in England, a woman was not only the head of a great and powerful nation, Queen Victoria was also the ruler of a vast empire. But this was Boston, and women of the day knew their places.

Outwardly, in all respects Martha toed the line, so to speak, and she did take on the staid and respectable air of the matrons of her new city and country. But privately, self-assured Martha became, albeit discreetly, completely immersed in all aspects of the bank that her husband ran. And it all happened quickly.

The Montagues had been in residence only a short time when Martha quietly became the prime mover in the affairs of the bank. Herbert at first objected to what he called 'meddling', but being of a nature that preferred peace in his house—and in his business—and rather on the slack side, his interests, if he were to admit it, lay elsewhere.

And the bank prospered.

No doubt about it, the reason the bank prospered was entirely due to Martha's business astuteness and in part because of her taking advantage of a boom that preceded the Civil War. As time went by, the bank continued to thrive by leaps and bounds, not the least of reasons being that even though she seemed for all intents and purposes the most conservative of women, Martha was a risk-taker.

And the bank prospered.

So much so that after fewer than five years in Boston, a magnificent building was constructed at the top of the main street to be the new bank. The house that the Montague's occupied was at the other end of the same street.

The great hall of the bank was fashioned after Saint Paul's Cathedral in London, England, with a huge dome dominating a circular ground floor plan. Pillars stretched from the floor up to just under the dome opening. Terrazzo tiles surrounded the entire lower walls; beige stonework reached to the ceiling. Huge oaken beams supported the tellers' cages. The dozens of doors leading off the hall were also made from the same aged English oak. At the far end, away from the main entrance, a great staircase twined up both sides of the hall to the floor above.

Yes, Martha made all the important decisions. And in the fullness of time, Herbert was not discontent to have it so. He preferred his cigars and brandy. Martha allowed him his occasional indulgences and peccadillos without complaint, as long it was done in moderation and, of course, with discretion. It was all very much between Martha and Herbert.

Outwardly and to everyone, he was in absolute command of the bank. And to the general public, he was, without doubt, the man in charge of a fine institution. And it came about that the magnificent bank building itself became an important landmark of the great city.

Martha was perfectly content with the way it had all turned out and wanted no public recognition whatsoever. So it suited both of them admirably. And even though it was a matter not for discussion for those employed at the bank, the bank's depositors and customers, or anyone else for that matter—public or private—people knew who really ran the show.

For more than five decades, Monday to Friday, at precisely ten forty-five a.m., Martha would be driven in her carriage from the house to the bank, now called the Montague Boston Bank. There she was entrenched in an office adjacent to that of her husband, doing who knew what until she re-enter the carriage at precisely two forty-five p.m. to return to the house at the other end of Beacon Street.

At the beginning of the sixth decade of her journey to the bank and back, Martha was driven by automobile for Martha kept up with, and was every now and then, ahead of the times. The only intervals when she would not make the trip was early in her marriage, when she was giving birth to her two sons and one daughter.

The Montagues would not leave America until they made what was known then as the 'Grand Tour'. The trip lasted a little more than two months in 1903 and was in celebration of their fiftieth wedding anniversary.

As the years went by, the bank not only grew in status. The people of Boston looked on the building itself with reverence and affection. It seemed as though there was not a time when the Montague Bank of Boston had not been there. It was indeed a grand edifice of integrity and strength.

And then there was Martha herself. People called Martha—not to her face, of course, but she knew it only too well—'The Old Lady'. Later, the bank itself took on that title. So it was time-honored over those many years, which ever way people thought and talked about it—be it Martha in her lifetime and later the bank itself—it was, forever and always, The Old Lady.

CHAPTER 19

Zero Minus Thirteen Hours

So far, this had been the easiest part of their trek. Shortly after leaving the underground river, they arrived at a part of the shaft where Steve indicated they would have to dig. Once more he set up the light desk, found a rock to sit on, and he and Mark began to confirm their position against the calculations and measurements.

This took only a brief time, and Mark and Johnny soon began digging into the rough wall with the aid of a small mechanical pick. The tiny machine took good-sized chunks out of the earth with each bite. Here, the ground was softer, and the little machine functioned well.

Luke and Matt dragged the muck, on plastic drop sheets, away from the area in which they now worked. After the first hour of this they changed, Steve and Luke dug while Mark and Johnny cleared away the diggings.

Steve had decided to rest Matt as much as possible, against Matt's protest that he was quite all right. His protests were, however, token, it seemed to the others. The old man looked very much the worse for wear. Matt quickly found a certainly not comfortable but tolerable spot. He almost immediately fell into a, if not deep sleep, at least a solid slumber.

As for the others, they, too, were drawing on extra reserves of energy. They had been down there for many hours, and none of those hours could be called easy. Now they were all beginning to show signs of real physical fatigue.

Steve paced the work so they could keep going steadily without exhausting them completely. He called a complete halt when the new hole was just under seven feet long.

They ate, and then they rested.

Less than an hour later, they were back at work. The hole quickly became longer.

Matt rejoined the work and, along with Luke, was shoring up some sections of the walls with almost paper-thin, light pieces of strong metal, metal similar to what is used in the manufacture of airplane fuselages and wings.

He placed each connecting piece neatly with the next one to form a square at about every two feet. The routine began to seem endless. Dig, change places, drag, rest, drink, eat, and rest. Dig, drag, rest, hour after hour.

Steve seemed to be holding up best, physically and mentally. He thought it quite possible that the minds of the others might begin to wander a little with mental weariness. So he kept a careful watch, ready to stop the work as soon as he could see any of them faltering. And so he called a halt to the work what seemed like every now and again for brief rest periods.

They continued in this way until Johnny, who under Steve's instructions had been digging upwards for more than an hour, shouted from the end of the tunnel. Steve crawled along quickly to find Johnny scraping dirt away from a great concrete mass over his head.

'Say this is it,' Johnny said. 'Please! Please, say this is it!'

'Yes, Johnny', he answered after carefully examined the concrete roof. 'That's it.'

'Thank Christ,' Johnny said. He let the air out of his lungs with a great sigh.

123

'Okay, clear away about three feet square of it, and then come on out. Okay?'

'Got it,' Johnny answered, a renewed strength in his voice.

Steve crawled back through and went over to where Matt was resting. 'This part of it is your baby, Matt.'

'Right.'

'I'll give you a hand if you don't feel up to it.'

'It'll take more than that little dunking back there to beat me. No, thanks. I won't need any help once I get my gear in there,' the old man said, rallying to give Steve as much confidence in his physical reserves as he could.

'All right, Matt. Johnny will be through in there soon, so whenever you're ready.'

Matt was already taking some packages from his backpack, then some wiring, and a small metal box.

The tunnel had taken twenty-seven hours, thirty-one minutes to dig, and all of them looked like they were ready to collapse from the effort. Steve noted this and everything else as he waited for Matt to bring his gear and enter the small square hole that had taken such a toll on their energy.

'I'm ready to go in now, Steve,' Matt said, approaching the entrance.

'Fine. You're sure? If you want,—'

'Just bring this backpack up after me,' he interrupted. He did not want any further discussion about his physical condition.

'Okay.'

Steve crawled up after Matt. When Matt was in position, kneeling under the concrete roof, Steve pushed the backpack up to his feet. Then Steve crawled back down and out of the hole.

Matt reappeared one hour and ten minutes later, carefully uncoiling wires as he emerged from the hole. 'She's all set, Steve.'

Steve stared at the tired old man for a long moment. Then, quite sure Matt had done his job, turned to the others. 'Now we all rest, but really rest! For the next part of the operation it is crucial that everyone be at the best possible peak of fitness. I know that's not so easy after what you've been through, but our success depends on it.'

'How will we wake up?' Mark asked. 'Suppose we oversleep.'

'That's not going to be a problem,' Steve replied as he noted that his watch told him they were forty-three hours and three minutes into the operation.

They were all fairly quiet for a while. Some of them were thinking about what they had gone through and what lay ahead. The only sounds were when they shuffled around, getting into as comfortable a position as they could in such a place. They rested but didn't sleep. Then, along with the others, Luke and Matt talked quietly about nothing in particular. Matt joked, 'I should have brought a book with me.'

'Seems to me like you've read an awful lot of books.'

'Oh, I guess I have,'

'You know, there's something I never really thought about before.'

'What's that Luke?' Matt asked softly, not to disturb the others if they were trying to sleep. But like them, they rested yes, but they were really too tired to sleep.

'Well, it's like this. I never saw my father with a book in his hand. A beer, sure, but never with a book. He knew where the library was in town, but he wouldn't know what the inside looked like. Yet he was well informed about almost everything. I suppose it was everything that he thought mattered anyway, world events, local stuff, things like that.'

'Interesting.'

'My dad was a big guy, big and very strong. He worked hard all his life, and the guys he worked with were pretty much the same. Tough, you know, regular guys, hard-working guys all their lives. Good guys, you know. Oh, sure, they would bitch about it. And he bitched too. But they really loved their jobs.'

Luke stopped talking for a minute and just shook his head, thinking about times gone by. Then he continued, 'I guess he was disappointed that I was small, you know? For being so short and skinny, not like him, big and tough. But he never showed it or said anything about it. He'd say, "Everyone's different, Luke. Everyone has different strengths."'

'He was right. Absolutely right. Sounds like a wise man.'

'Yeah, he was.' Luke shook his head again. He seemed to grin in a peculiar way, as though trying to put into words what had remained stored in his mind for a long time. 'He was just a guy, I guess, but you know, in some way he was a great man. Oh, I don't mean that he invented something or saved the world kind of thing. I don't know. Maybe he was a great man in a small way. You know, he helped a lot of people, never turned down anyone for a favor. Like never. Yeah, he helped a lot of people. And he died broke because of it, but I know for sure that's the way he would want it. My mother would just say okay if he gave money to someone to help them out, knowing for sure they would never see it again. And he would be broke again. But you know what? I can't remember my dad having an unhappy day, you know that? Not once.'

'That's a fine memory to have, Luke.'

'Seemed like they got old before their time. My mom and dad were like old young people, huh? I guess that makes no sense.'

'You are wrong, Luke. It makes a lot of sense.'

'You think? Well, anyway.' Luke sighed.

'Did he work at—'

'No, but he helped me get the job. He liked the idea of me working hard. Well, you know, not at a desk kind of job. And I know he was always proud of me. I hated it there at Massey Remolds. They treated me like shit from the get-go.' Luke nodded. 'But I learned a lot.' His voice changed to a softer tone. 'I was there nine freakin' years before I told them to shove it and left. Guess that's all over now.'

'Yes.'

'I know that makes no sense either.'

Matt smiled. 'You have beautiful thoughts, Luke.'

'Well anyway, I guess I'm like him. He sure never would hurt anyone, and me too. And I hope no one gets hurt, you know, in what we're doing with this.'

'If everything goes to plan, no one will get hurt,' Matt assured him.

Luke sighed and let out a small guffaw. 'Huh, my old man, huh! A great man? Well, what the hell? I like to think of him as a great man.'

'Then he was.'

There was another spell of quiet.

'That's weird. I don't even know why I said any of that.'

'Memories, Luke, they are with us forever. And I guess some of them can seem weird when viewed from a distance.'

Mark had been listening, and now he joined in the conversation. 'You want to hear something really weird?'

Johnny groaned. 'Oh, Jesus, he's going to sing. That's right, guys, he sings some weird stuff about mad girls.'

'Madrigals, old boy, madrigals.'

'Whatever. It's weird shit. It's about as musical as a bull farting through a comb.'

'Anyway. I'm not going to sing. What I was going to say was about my stepmother. I had a stepmother. Our family had been farming for generations. You know, back in England. My mother died when I was only about ten, and a couple of years later, my dad married a woman who already had two daughters who were both a lot older than me.' He laughed sardonically. 'And man, that woman turned out to be a real hellcat. The girls were just as bad, maybe even worse. Really, I mean they were really nasty people. Those big stepsisters were tough on me. It got so bad my dad sent me to a boarding school. And since I never wanted to be a farmer, that was fine with me. I couldn't get away soon enough.'

His voice softened. 'My father passed away when I was at university. The farm and everything else would have passed on to me. But when he married, that all changed. She got half, and I got

127

half of everything, the farm and the house. They made it impossible for me to live there, not that I wanted to. The widow was a lunatic and the two daughters full-blown bitches. I never went back to the house.'

He paused for a minute then went on. 'Well, as it turned out, she had been seeing this lawyer on the side, and they got together and schemed. And believe it or not, she sued me for my share of the estate. When the case came to court, I had no money to speak of. I had just finished my degree and was looking for a job. A lawyer said he would represent me on some kind of contingency basis, but after he looked into the thing, he said the widow would probably win. So he dumped me.

'When I showed up in court, the judge asked if I had a lawyer. I said I would represent myself. You know, pro se. He didn't like that, but the widow did. I was on the ropes and on the way to losing, and I knew it. So what do you think I did?'

'No idea,' Matt said. Luke shook his head.

'I gave my share of the estate to her daughters.'

'I don't get it,' Matt asked.

'Yeah. Why did you do that?' Luke wanted to know.

'I had a pretty good idea of what would happen. See, I knew those people and what they would probably do—something unprincipled.'

'What?' Luke wanted to know.

Matt scratched the back of his neck. 'I have no guess. 'Okay, what?'

'The daughters sued their mother,'

'They did?' Luke shook his head incredulously. 'That's terrible.'

'Oh yes, they were terrible people,' Mark declared. And then he laughed. 'To tell the truth, it wasn't much of a farm anymore. It wasn't big enough for any commercial use and too small really to make a living from. Just a place to live.'

'But a daughter suing a mother, that is unbelievable,' Luke said. 'Even worse, the two of them.'

'Yep, the daughters sued their mother for the whole estate, and the old girl sued them right back.'

Matt nodded. 'Ah, I think I know the outcome, or make a good guess.'

'Okay?'

'The lawyers got it all by way of legal fees. Right?'

'Well', Mark said, 'I don't know about that. I guess that is what could happen. I wouldn't be surprised if the case is still going on.' Mark laughed again. 'Last I heard, they were still fighting. But that was a long time ago. I really don't know.' He snorted. 'Or care.'

'Then maybe the lawyers will sue whoever wins,' Matt opined.

'Huh! That would be a dream come true.'

'No doubt about it,' Matt said, 'greed will change the shape of a person's mind.'

No one said anything for a time.

Then Luke broke the silence. 'Matt.'

'Yes?'

'What the hell is the motley?'

Matt laughed. 'Oh, the motley.'

'Yeah. You said, "On with the motley."'

'Sure. Well, it means a lot of things. Shakespeare says it at times. It can mean a set of clothes, and a clown's get-up. Let's see, and yes, it can mean a diverse group of people, you know, like us. But mostly it means on with the show. That's was the way I meant it, you know. Let's get on with it, on with the show. Okay?'

'Yep, got it.'

They fell silent for a few minutes until Luke spoke again.

'Matt, you know when I hear you put words together sometimes, and stuff from books, too, I mean things I never heard before, well I …' He stopped.

'Go on, Luke.'

'Well, I know you're going to laugh at this, but …' He hesitated again.

'Yes.'

'Okay, see the thing is, there was always something I wanted to do. I kind of had the feeling that I'd like to take a whack, well, at writing.' He stopped for a second and looked at Matt through the gloom of their surroundings. 'I told you you'd laugh.'

'Not at all, Luke. I can't see why not.'

'First off, I don't have the education for it.'

'Education is only part of it,' Matt scoffed. 'Sure, some education is necessary, of course, reading and writing. But the rest of writing comes from many things—experience, instinct, and most of all, I suppose, from the heart. And about education, Mark Twain left school at the age of twelve, so he couldn't have had much in the way of formal education.'

'I guess not. See, that's the kind of thing I know nothing about. And another thing, I have sort of mixed-up ideas of what I want to write about, or who I want to write about. You know, it's just that I think about it and wonder if I—'

Matt interrupted, 'I think you could be a good writer, Luke. Writing is just an extension of thinking. And you are a thinker, so you should give it a shot.'

'Really?'

'Absolutely. And remember I said I had a book for you? The fact is I have several that I think would be a great help to you. Not how to write; no one can really teach you if you don't have something of your own inside.'

'Okay, thanks.'

'You won't know if you can unless you try. I say go for it, Luke!'

'You know something? That's part of the reason I'm down here, doin' this now. Like I might have some money, and that way I could do as I pleased. You know?'

'Like I said, we all have our reasons.'

'I guess I could come up with something in the way of a story. But what? Hmm.'

'Writing doesn't have to be about big stuff. You could write about your dad.'

'Yeah, never thought about that. I could. My dad was a great guy, and he did a lot of stuff.'

'Good stories are really about interesting people doing interesting things in interesting places.'

'Matt, you know what?' Luke set his jaw and nodded forcefully. 'I'm going to do it!'

'Good for you!'

They were quiet again for several minutes, Then Luke reopened the conversation on a slightly different theme. 'Matt, okay if I ask you something else?'

'Shoot.'

'Why are you doing it?'

'Good question. You're asking that because I'm old, right?'

'Well ...'

'That's okay, Luke. I guess we're all pondering that about each other. It's easy to say that everyone has his reasons and move on. And I guess that's enough. Why? Yes, why? Hmm, to be rich? No. To be a somebody? Definitely no.'

'Yeah, but still, why this?'

Matt shifted his eyes so that he was not really looking at any of them, more like he was looking around them and deliberating whether he would answer the question. And then deciding that he would, declared in a quiet, unhurried voice.

'All right, let's see. I'll try and put it, you know, from where I stand. Well, the years pass without you really taking notice. Then one day you wake up to find that somehow, you've been stuffed into this old man's body, and you wonder when that happened. Then you begin to wonder what's next. Then you think maybe, maybe nothing's next. And the fact that you're old kind of hits you in the kisser.' He smiled at that. Then Matt became more serious. 'And then, on reviewing your current existence, you realize that your life has been reduced to playing solitaire and boring people with tedious homilies and writings of ancient men, perhaps with words that have little meaning in a modern world. And that's about when you start to believe—*to know*—that you're only doing it to hide your unchanging aloneness.'

Matt shook his head a little. A wry smile tiptoed onto his face. 'The winters seem to be colder and the summers hotter. And you wonder if soon you'll start to believe that nothing really matters anymore.'

Matt went silent for a few moments. Then he murmured softly, almost to himself, 'And then there's something you never want to have to say when you're closer to the end than the beginning. And that is, "I wish I had done that."'

Matt took a breath and concluded his answer to Luke's question. 'Maybe, for me anyway, that's why.' He smiled at something in his head. 'The what used to be won't come back.'

There was complete silence as the others were deep in their own thoughts.

Matt was thinking, too, wondering if he would ever learn to keep his big mouth shut. 'I think we should …' Then he let go with a long sigh. As the sigh tailed off, he added, 'Get some rest.'

Zero hour was six hours, fifty-seven minutes away.

CHAPTER 20

Rupert's Plan

Rupert Brady Montague was not really a complicated man. However, he did have two exceedingly dissimilar personalities. The outer character, the one everyone saw, was one in which he presented himself as competently businesslike coupled with a substantial measure of self-importance. Not overly gracious but, in general, reasonably affable.

The other character, the one no one saw, was a Rupert who carried a significant measure of animosity, an animosity that was buried quite deep, thoroughly masked, and had several levels ranging from simple dislike through the grades of aversion, going all the way to out-and-out hatred.

Among his minor dislikes was his given name, Rupert. He didn't like it. So for those times when he met new people, usually ladies—he liked the ladies—he used Monty. And now that he was at odds with his wife, Monty was frequently his pseudonym of choice. Also, when away from the bank in non-business situations, he avoided using the name of Montague, preferring to let his money do the talking.

At the moment, Rupert disliked his wife. They had been married for more than ten years. But the marriage had, for all intents and purposes, started to crumble after the first couple of years. He now believed now that she only married him for the money and the prestige of the family name. And, of course, the bank. He saw her as an elitist and a socialite. But that was no surprise, and anyway, he was himself quite snobbish.

Constance spent a good deal of the time nowadays at a house she bought in Newport, Long Island, New York, where she hobnobbed with other socialites. Then she wintered in Palm Springs, Florida, with others of the same stripe. For her part, she started to think of him as a inadequate husband and selfish lover. If that wasn't enough, in everyday things, she found him to be petty and mean. Not with everyone, certainly, but certainly with her.

From about two years into the marriage, Rupert and Constance had begun to lead somewhat separate lives. Both were discontented that the marriage was now not much more than a show, but neither seemed willing to do anything to change, or at least improve the situation.

He also now believed that he only married at the insistence of his parents, who had suggested strongly that he should do so. Nowadays, Rupert longed for the single life that he never had. The life of the playboy and the lothario that he, at times, imagined himself to be.

He often thought things would be different had he held out a little longer before bowing to his parents' wishes because his father was now no longer involved in the bank. Rupert had been in control for some years.

His mother never had any interest in the bank. These days, she was utterly engrossed in her garden to the exclusion of everything else.

Constance's residence was, of course, the Boston mansion. But the time she spent there now seemed to be guided around some social events in the city, which meant that she and Rupert didn't have to spend a lot of time together.

Rupert also lived in the house, of course, but some of his nights were spent in an apartment he owned in one of the luxury blocks in the city. Both of them tried to limit the time they spent together to obligatory social occasions that could not be avoided. They were civil to each other when in the company of others, so their mutual hostility usually went unnoticed. They had two children, both girls. Rupert wondered if his daughters would turn out to be like their mother.

The thing was that he did love her at the beginning, and he was sure that she loved him. But now, they went out of their way to rankle each other. They knew, of course, that what they were doing was foolish and not a good thing for the children, but they couldn't seem to stop.

Although his inner character told him that he disliked Constance, he was not opposed to the idea of the occasional bedroom romp with her when they were both at the house. After all, she was very beautiful and kept herself in great shape, partly the result of a personal trainer's know-how and, of course, her beautician. But then again, Constance was a natural beauty, and there was no doubt that she was gifted with immense sexual attraction.

Mostly she would turn him down at the first advance, but she sometimes went along with it if she was in the mood. This even though she had convinced herself he was a poor performer.

The fact was, they were stuck with each other, and they would never divorce. It was not a question of money. Constance was quite wealthy in her own right. And the dividends from the shares she owned in the Montague Bank gave her a handsome independent income.

His parents were at first disappointed that the marriage seemed to be a flop. They didn't seem to care so much anymore. Mother Montague had this obsessive interest in orchids and spent her waking hours in a large hothouse on the grounds of the estate. The senior Montague, who was at one time an astute and clever businessman, now took interest in nothing. Rupert thought of his father as old and annoying, and they didn't get along very well these days.

Rupert was in full control of the bank, but in reality, it was Cyrus Bishop, the general manager, who ran every aspect of the Boston Montague Bank. He had been there from when he was a boy. His first job was as office boy and runner. Then he became an assistant cashier and so on up as the years passed. He was at the Montague Bank in Rupert's grandfather's—old John Montague— time. He had begun at the very bottom and had done every dreary job on his way up the ladder to where he was now—the boss. All but one.

Curiously, in the middle range of Rupert's dislikes was Martha, his long-gone great-great-grandmother, Martha Brady Montague. Beautiful, charitable, decent Martha worked so selflessly to make the bank into something from the little nothing it was when she first arrived in Boston. Martha had been the one who brought the bank to the solid institutional status it was today. And it was notable that there was not one foreclosure during her entire duration at the bank. Compassionate Martha always found a way to help people out of their financial difficulties, contrary to most bankers of the day.

Rupert often thought that he would like to drop the Brady part of his name. The history of the 'Old Lady' thing was distasteful to him. The idea of an old woman coming to the bank every day seemed absurd to him. Why was the thought of Martha so distasteful to him? He convinced himself that it was because Martha Baker had come from low class; Rupert scorned her for her common roots. It seemed, even to his inner character, that he disliked everything today. Nothing pleased him anymore. He just wanted to get out.

Out and away.

Rupert knew that he wasn't the most handsome man in the world, but he thought of himself as being reasonably attractive to women. In fact, he was not that bad-looking. No, it was his assertive and conceited demeanour that was really offensive. His saving grace was that he was generous when it came to the ladies.

He was not afraid to open his wallet and that made him, if not exactly alluring, at least endurable to some women. What difference did it make, he would persuade himself, with women? You could get away with anything if you had money.

His plan—and he had planned for several years—was perfect. He would eventually leave Boston altogether. He would go to live in a place like Switzerland or France. Live the life of a rich man in a foreign country. Perhaps Italy or the French Riviera. He had been to the French Riviera and liked it. In Europe, they knew how to treat the rich. Anyway, he thought, if you're rich, you don't have to live in just one place; he could have two or three residences. Since Boston fell easily into his dislike category he would not miss the city.

This was top secret, of course. No one would have guessed what was really in his mind. He would be gone one day, and they could all, 'Kiss my derriere!' That is everyone—the family, his wife, huh! His friends. Well, he had few real friends.

Obviously, he would keep control of the bank. Cyrus Bishop and the general management did all the grunt work anyway, so he would not be missed. With easy communications, it would be simple to live anywhere in the world and still be the man in charge.

Yes, he had thought it all out.

And there was another thing. Cyrus Bishop was getting to be more and more of a pain in the ass. Bishop enjoyed nothing better than to call a meeting and propose some trivial innovation for the bank. And he had all kinds of trifling ideas about improving the bank's procedures and others, less trifling, about expansion. It was typically a number of things that held no interest for Rupert. In fact, Rupert wanted the bank to stay as it was and to change nothing. But he really left it all up to Bishop. It made everything easier for him. The bank was profitable, running smoothly, and for the most part, Rupert could stay out of the way. He could be Monty full-time.

As for Bishop himself, Rupert wanted nothing more than to see him gone. But that was never going to happen. He was not really close to retirement age, and anyway, Bishop knew the banking business better than anyone. Another thing, he had been loyal and served the bank and, therefore, the Montague family very well all those years.

All that was well and good. But Rupert did not like him and never had. Not for anything really, and yet for everything. Just for being Cyrus Bishop. Bishop was unequivocally professional, correct in every possible way, and compliant to Rupert. And always ingratiating to him, just as he was to Rupert's father and grandfather. Yet Rupert found him enduringly irritating.

Regardless of the irritation he caused Rupert, there was no doubt about his ability to run the bank. There was no one better in the business. Bishop loved the banking business, and he loved the Montague Bank more than anything in the world. He got the job done. Besides, if he were to get rid of Bishop, Rupert's plan would be harder to pull off.

No, Bishop was as permanent as the limestone bricks that held the bank up. But he was a pain in the ass that Rupert would not miss when he put his plan into place.

Yes, Rupert had many dislikes. But his big dislike now was saved for the bank itself. That stretched all the way back. He disliked the bank more than anything, yet money was the lifeblood of his plan.

And not just money, cash money. Several years ago, he started to skim off the top. Through a number of sharp deals and financial finagling, he was able to accumulate a large amount of money that he had separated from the bank. He did keep *his* money in the bank vault, but that was purely for convenience, until he could move it to where he wanted it in Europe. The money itself was separated from any other stacks and boxes of cash.

Like other banking institutions, most business was done via electronic transfers and such. But this money, gained by way of those several machinations and financial schemes, was his. It was his getaway money—forty million dollars—in cash!

Rupert visited his money almost every day that he was in the bank. Stacked flawlessly neat in a large steel cabinet, row upon row, with the amount of each bundle printed clearly on the tape holding it together. In just a few minutes, he could scan and count the money without even moving one of the stacks.

The cabinet with its piles of currency occupied a small area at the far end of the huge vault. It would be easy to move when he was ready. Rupert would smile as he looked on all that money. It was definitely a thing of undeniable omnipotent excellence.

The bank's cash money was near the front of the vault to be taken to the tills and smaller safes for the day-to-day transactions. But *his* money was never touched by anyone but him.

His getaway was always on Rupert's mind. Refining and rearranging the details of how he would go about the departure. Over time, he flirted with several ideas, such as changing his name or buying a fake passport and other documents. Would it be legal? If not, so what? But then why? There would be no need for any of that. He could do as he pleased. With money you can do anything you want. So there it sat, waiting for his getaway.

Forty million dollars—cash!

CHAPTER 21

A House by the Sea

The Wheelers were a comfortably off but hardly well-to-do family who lived in the town of Cape May, on the southernmost tip of New Jersey, nestled between the Delaware Bay and the Atlantic Ocean.

He was the first, and what turned out to be their only child, arriving late in their marriage. John and Evelyn had been married fourteen years when he was born. A son—a thrill beyond measure—they named Steven.

John Wheeler ran a local hardware store. While it could not be described as a booming business, it afforded them a comfortable living. They lived in a large old house on the edge of the Atlantic Ocean. The house was made entirely of various hardwoods brought over from England almost two centuries before. It had a splendid interior of light oak panelling throughout, and a winding staircase made of darker mahogany. It was a substantial and solidly built, three-storey structure, standing as it did in noble defiance of the vagaries of a powerful sea.

Yes, the house had been there for a long time. Strangely, it looked like it had always been there—as the sea itself had been there—and that it should always be there.

Steve's great-grandfather bought the house from the widow of one of the many sea captains who plied their trade in the then-booming sailing days. The house was old, and naturally, with the passage of time and being so close to the sea, it was in constant need of upkeep. Even though John Wheeler spent most of the time running the hardware store, he was well up to the task. So the house was always in good repair, not withstanding its great age.

The house was, in its way, undeniably a landmark. It could be seen from almost everywhere in the town, as well as from the ships that sailed out of Philadelphia and other ports along the south-eastern seaboard. From a distance, the house looked rather magnificent, sitting precariously as it did on a spit of land that jutted out into the sea.

The house had the usual layout—first-floor living rooms and kitchen; the second floor bedrooms and a bathroom that featured a huge, white bathtub sitting on four big ornamental legs. On the top floor there were two maids' rooms. Above that was access to the widow's walk.

The widow's walk was a narrow walkway on which the wives of seamen could stand and watch for their husbands' ships to appear after a long voyage in the perilous sailing days. Many houses in Cape May had a widow's walk.

In the Wheeler house, a narrow stairway ran from the top floor hallway up to this little chamber that measured only a few feet across and had a low ceiling. It was furnished with a tiny table, a small lounge seat that had to have been assembled in the room, and a chair hardly big enough for a child or small woman. There was an old oil lamp that had been refitted with an electric bulb.

To a little boy growing up in a house like that was a daily adventure. Steve loved the whole house, but his favorite part was the widow's walk. From the time Steve could toddle, he was allowed to go up to the widow's walk alone.

Steve spent hour upon hour in the little chamber on top of the house, conjuring in his mind stories of pirate lore and adventure while gazing out over the ever-changing blue sea. During a storm, he sometimes climbed the twisting stairway to watch the storm's ferocity brought to his very window in the form of waves of white-capped mountains of water threshing to shore.

Cape May was a clean, orderly, well-kept town. Residents took pride in their tranquil community. However, in summer, the character of this picturesque place on the ocean changed dramatically. Beachfront hotels that had remained silent and shuttered during winter months opened to an influx of summer guests taken care of by mostly out-of-town workers, maids, and cooks. All manner of seasonal help came to the little place that, for around ten weeks, became a summer resort. Everything and everyone who lived in Cape May changed with the seasons. Steve loved each of the seasons as they came in turn.

He always thought that when he was grown, he would work with his hands and body, doing hard work. He was strong with lots of energy. Reading, writing, and the rest of it at school were, to his mind, something you had to endure before getting on with the real job of living. Yet he liked school well enough, and he got on well with teachers and other students. Making friends came easily to Steve.

The excitement of the summer months held many pleasures for Steve. The summer people were coming back. He loved to go down and watch the workmen take hundreds of shutters off the sleeping behemoths that were the stately Congress Hall Hotel and the elegant Chalfont Hotel. To see the carnival people putting up the rides and repainting for the hundredth time the boardwalk shops. And the carnival atmosphere that pervaded the entire beachfront and town was, for Steve and everyone who lived in Cape May, the most exciting time of the year.

Rich Philadelphia families came to Cape May for their summer vacations. The large houses they owned lay like slumbering giants awaiting the arrival of, for perhaps the hundredth time, the owners and old retainers. They usually brought with them a new member born between summer seasons, commencing a tradition of their own.

Warm water and summer breezes lured many from the hot, dusty city that few could resist. No doubt about it, with the coming of summer, life changed for everyone at Cape May.

The Wheeler house had guests too. Steve's aunt Trish and uncle Mack would arrive punctually on the day preceding Memorial Day, train tickets having been purchased far in advance. They would leave the day following Labor Day.

Aunt Trish was a lady from the old school, brought up in a structured middle-class household. She was a stern and unadorned person. Standing or sitting, she always assumed a perfect posture—erect and correct. She never seemed to relax, as if to do so would be a letdown of her standards and propriety. She was a good woman, of course, but not someone a little boy surrounded by deep affection would easily warm to. But Steve did.

Aunt Trish's husband, Mack, was totally different. He was easy-going and friendly with a ready wit. He never seemed to mind that his wife was of an unusually stern nature. And he was far from being the nagged husband. On the contrary, they got on remarkably well with each other, an understanding reached long ago and meticulously adhered to by both these good people of such diverse characters.

The only other member of the household was Ruby, the maid who had been with the Wheelers since they were married and moving into the house on the day of the wedding. She was from a large family in Pleasantville, near Atlantic City. Ruby lived in the top rooms of the house.

In summer, John would, from time to time, leave the store in the care of the workers, and he and Steve went sailing in the Wheeler's eighteen-foot boat. They would leave the house very early, after a solid breakfast, and return in time for lunch around noon.

Steve loved this part of the summer. If Uncle Mack were there, he sometimes went with them, even though he was not all that keen on little boats.

Other times, Steve and Mack sat fishing on one of the docks. Mack was always great fun to be with; he knew just about everything.

He had been quite a wanderer in his younger days, before he married, and would relate stories of foreign places to Steve's eager ears. He told of things that Steve would never forget. And later, he would reflect on those stories. Steve realized his uncle was really a philosopher of great perception and humour, never absolutely separating one from the other.

From when the age of seven, Steve worked at the store, fetching and carrying the same as the other workers. When things were really busy, he even waited on customers. He liked that the best. Polite, never shy, he related well to almost anyone. Even the rare grouchy shopper would relent at the open-faced smile and genuine friendly attitude of the bright little boy. The money he earned was to be saved sensibly and spent foolishly on summer rides and amusements.

Labor Day ended the season officially. It would be as though some giant hand pressed a button to make it all disappear. One day crowds of people; the next, they would all be gone. Gone, too, were the rides and amusements that had seemed so permanently a part of the land, simply pulled down during the night and taken away.

Nature's sounds of waves and seabirds took the place of loudspeakers blaring out their music and messages of wonder and delight, backed up by the pipe organ music of the carousel.

The next day, Steve would go down to the boardwalk and listen to the sounds that weren't there anymore, feeling alone and abandoned. And he would cry. A little boy sitting there crying because everyone, even his wonderful Uncle Mack and Aunt Trish, had gone away and left him. The emptiness he felt at those times never really left him.

After sitting there for a time, he would begin to wander slowly and aimlessly more or less in the direction of home. When the big, old, wooden house came into view, his step would quicken. Then he would break into a wild run for the rest of the way.

He ran straight into the kitchen, his too small arms trying to encircle the huge black package of love and friendship that was Ruby. His true dear friend for ten months of the year. He would abandon her for others at the beginning of summer, and he would faithfully and unashamedly return to her at summer's end. Dear, beautiful Ruby would accept his renewed attention without hesitation, even though he had hardly noticed her during the summer weeks.

Ruby was not the only black person living in a white household in Cape May. But most who worked as help lived in their own houses at that time. Black families were accepted in Cape May.

Ruby loved all the Wheelers, especially Mrs Evelyn Wheeler, whom she called Miss Evy. Miss Evy had, from the beginning, treated her more like a sister than a maid, and Ruby knew she never wanted to be anywhere but where she was.

John and Evelyn Wheeler took a sort of vacation at summer's end each year. John opened the store at the usual time but closed earlier during September to accommodate the limited business at that time. The family took an occasional trip to Philadelphia or Atlantic City. Sometimes they just lazed around the house, catching up on reading.

And sailing the eighteen-footer, something the sailing enthusiast John Wheeler loved to do at that time of year. It was still warm in the sunshine, but brisk, quick breezes allowed the boat to zip along at a wild pace. Evelyn was, like Uncle Mack, not keen on the boat but went along sometimes. After all, she knew how much her husband enjoyed sailing.

And so the seasons passed for Steve at Cape May. Fall, winter, spring, and summer, each season brought with it its own wondrous change, and yet a certain unchangeability prevailed in the happy years of his childhood. The unchanging world he knew, his parents, caring, and to him, perpetual. Uncle Mack and Aunt Trish arriving and departing with the punctuality of the seasons themselves. And loving, gentle Ruby, his friend forever.

And then there was the thing that embodied all those things—the house itself. The great, wonderful house that stood fast for all those years through the violent storms of winter and the blistering heat of summer. Strong and sturdy, it would be there forever, and so would he. Steve loved his house.

Steve was still in school that afternoon when dark clouds began to appear, and the wind rattled the louvered windows of the schoolroom. A sudden and unexpected weather system brought on a violent storm to a day that began with bright sunshine and a soft breeze.

By the time school let out, it was raining hard. A blustery wind tried to knock him off his feet as he raced home. In the kitchen, Ruby rubbed his head dry with a towel till his ears rang. Then she sent him upstairs to change into dry clothes.

The Wheelers had gone out in the boat that morning and not yet returned. It was not that unusual for them to be late as John often said that sailboats have destinations but no ETAs. This unexpected storm changed everything.

Aunt Trish and Uncle Mack arrived the next night after the storm. There was no trying to comfort Steve because he didn't believe they were lost. So his aunt and uncle left him alone for the most part. He would go down to the little, now empty, jetty and wait for a while. Then he would go home and on to widow's walk to watch for a sail to round the breakwater. Waiting to see the little white hull bobbing over the harbour entrance current. Waiting for his mother and father to return to him.

But they did not come.

The bodies were recovered several days later, near one of the coves. They must have been trying to reach it and safety at the first sight of the gathering clouds. Of the little boat there was no sign. She must have overturned and sunk quickly as his parents struggled in the water to get to the shore. His mother and father were tied together in death by a rope, no doubt a last effort to keep them from being separated in the water.

Almost the entire town attended their funeral. All the storekeepers closed their businesses for the day out of respect for the loss of one of their most respected colleagues and his wife.

Steve was surprised to see his ordinarily austere aunt Trish crying at the churchyard but not to see tears flowing openly down the gentle face of his uncle Mack. Steve was dry-eyed that day, conscious only of the uncomfortable weight of the dark-blue serge suit and the unusual tightness of the buttoned-up shirt and black necktie. He accepted the kindly words and handshakes of the grown-ups without answering.

When it was over, he went back to the widow's walk and stayed there for the rest of the night. Ruby came up the tiny winding staircase once to be with him. But before she reached the room, she could hear a sobbing from the little boy that almost broke her heart. She didn't go any further. She simply slumped down there on the stairs, joining him in his lonely anguish for it was the saddest day of her life too.

Leaving the house a few days later was almost as big a loss to Steve as the loss of his parents. Steve was to go with Uncle Mack and Aunt Trish to live in Philadelphia.

Mack appointed one of the store's help to run it in the meantime, until the wills of Steve's parents could be probated. Mack had long ago been named executor of their estate should anything happen to them. Quite simply, except for a bequest to Ruby, everything was left to Steve—the store, the house, even the little boat that was no more. His father had life insurance too. Of course, the bank held a mortgage on both the store and house because of money borrowed to improve the store. But when everything was settled with the insurance company, both would be free of encumbrances. Even under new management, the store would provide enough to educate Steve, and money could be put by for his future.

Mack's house was not as big as the one at Cape May, but it was comfortable and roomy, with large bay windows in front and a good-sized yard at the back. It was set in a nice part of town but far off the Main Line. Steve's room was to the rear of the second floor. Though smaller than his at Cape May, it had a nice view and its own bathroom.

The first few weeks in Philadelphia brought with it awesome hurdles for Steve, enrolling in a new school, unable to roam where he pleased, missing his friends and having no desire to make new ones. All the while suffering the pain of the loss of his parents made him an unhappy, lonely little boy. And while his uncle and aunt treated him as their own son and were kind and gentle, he longed for the solitude of the widow's walk.

He gradually became more in tune with the faster-paced life in a big city and to become a member of a family again. After all, they were his only living relatives. And he loved Uncle Mack; there was a strong bond between them, though a different kind than with father and son, but still a bond. Aunt Trish was still righteously firm and of stern countenance, strict with him from the start. But she loved him more than her nature would allow her to show. And he knew that.

Not that long after the accident, a letter arrived from the insurance company that first astounded Mack and then brought out a rage in him that confirmed his wild Irish antecedents. It said, in insensitively brief terms, that the insurance was not payable because at the time the Wheelers went out in their boat, a small-craft advisory had already been issued. Therefore, they went at their own risk, so the insurance company was not liable; the policy was void. Of course Mack instructed a lawyer to protect Steve's rights, but all too soon it became apparent that what the company claimed was true.

A small-craft warning had been issued just forty minutes before the boat put to sea. But Mack wanted to know how the Wheelers were supposed to know about it. 'That's just it,' the lawyer explained, 'according to maritime law, boat owners must find out about the weather in advance of departing or go at their own risk.' He could fight, of course, but advised against it. Insurance companies play by their own rules and were undisposed to make payment if there was the slightest suggestion of any irregularity.

Steve and his uncle went back Cape May. The house was now closed and boarded up. And there was more bad news. The small bank the Wheelers used for so many years had gone bust and been taken over by some out-of-state bank, and it now owned the house, along with several other properties in and around Cape May. The people from that bank were there, touring those properties.

There were four of them. Steve recognized the old manager from the Cape May bank, Mr Bratten. He saw Steve, and sheepishly and quickly, he looked away. The other three were from out of town—the president of the other bank, his twenty-year-old son, and another man.

The father and son walked around until they came within earshot of Steve and his uncle, whom they ignored. 'Well, boy, what shall we do with this old house?'

'Burn it, Father,' the son replied and grinned. 'Burn it.'

'Burn the house, Rupert?'

'Sure.'

'Really?'

'Sure. It's just a big, old, heap of shit, so burn it.'

Turning to the other man, his father asked, 'What do you think, Bishop?'

The man at first shook his head but then nodded. 'The house is old and has little value.'

The young man was almost joyful. 'That's what I said,' he shouted. 'It's a heap of old shit, so burn it!'

But they didn't burn it.

A month later, Steve watched as a wrecking ball and bulldozers demolished the—his—house. The house that had stood there for almost two hundred years was gone in two hundred minutes.

Steve was told they intended to sell the land. But the land the house sat on for all those years lay fallow from then on. People were more careful and wary of the danger of being out there in the event of a hurricane or big storm.

The house he so loved was gone. He would only be able to wander its rooms and halls and seek the ultimate solitude of the widow's walk in his memory.

CHAPTER 22

Zero Hour Minus Twenty-One Minutes, Thirty Seconds: Are You Ready?

There was a lovely old clock above the door of Cyrus Bishop's office. And when it indicated five minutes to three, two uniformed bank guards appeared and stood waiting, one at each side of the doorway. A minute later, the door opened, and Mr Bishop, the second in charge of the Montague Bank of Boston, walked through. The portly, rich bank official checked the time on the big clock against his watch, briefly inspected the guards, and then headed to the staircase, the guards following several respectful paces behind him.

They negotiated down the winding staircase and arrived at the main vault at one minute to three. At precisely three o'clock, Mr Bishop nodded, and the guards, on his wordless order, swung shut the great steel door of the vault and turned the wheel, locking the bolts into position with a series of dull thuds.

Mr Bishop calmly smiled his approval. It was really just another part of the smooth running of a business, but Mr Bishop saw it as more than that. Yes, it meant the close of the business day. And yes, business still went on in the bank, but the closing of the great vault door was done with formality and style marking the long-standing tradition behind it. And again yes, Mr Bishop could indeed feel satisfied.

✦──────✦✦✦──────✦

Twenty or so feet below, tension had taken over the occupants of the tunnel. Perhaps even Steve was now nervous, but he was not alone in exhibiting some signs of uneasiness. Of the others, Matt exhibited quiet but alert readiness. Johnny and Mark showed few outward signs of nerves, but Steve could see that they were feeling the pressure. Only Luke had taken on an expression of actual fear. And he, feeling a nervous need to say something, leaned closer to Matt and prattled in the barely audible whispered, 'Man, am I glad to get out of here. The closest I ever want to get to hell.'

Matt could tell how Luke felt by his edgy and shaky voice. 'No hell, Luke,' Matt said matching only Luke's whisper. 'No hell below us, above us only sky.'

Luke brightened. 'Euripides, right?'

'Lennon.'

'The Russian dictator?'

'John Lennon, from his song "Imagine".'

'Oh, yeah. I know that one.'

'So Luke,' Mark looked over at him and spoke quietly, 'I was going to ask you about Massey Remolds and …'

'Yeah?'

Matt decided not to go any further when he noticed how badly Luke's hands were shaking. 'Skip it,' Mat said.

No doubt about it, all of them were jumpy. Even so, they seemed prepared for what was about to happen as they waited on Steve's orders.

'Supposing it isn't closed yet?' Johnny asked.

151

'Johnny', Steve answered without looking up from his watch, 'that vault door has been closed for two minutes and fifty seconds.'

'Are you sure?' Luke wanted to know.

'I'm sure,' Steve answered in a voice that was trying hard to instill calm in the youngest man. 'Matt?'

'Yes?'

'Are you ready?

Matt hesitated for a second before saying what Steve needed to hear. 'I'm ready. Yes, I'm ready, Steve.'

The old man looked much older now. He said quietly to Luke, who knelt beside him, 'This is going to make quite a bang. Yes, sir, quite a bang.'

Then he called again to Steve, only a little louder, 'We're ready, Steve!'

Are you ready?

It was the same question Kate had wondered about many times since early that morning. Just as important, she wondered if the others were ready. She had no way of knowing how far into the operation, as Steve insisted on calling it, had gotten, or whether perhaps they had not made it at all. That would mean all the ancillary arrangements were to go for nothing. Or even, she could hardly bring herself to accept the thought, that they might all be dead, lying there under the ground. Maybe they hadn't made it beyond the water tube. She had no way of knowing. And if it were to end right now, there was no way of knowing.

Are you ready?

Kate had questioned herself over and over. Had the others performed their parts? Perhaps one of them will fail or has already failed. Maybe even Steve himself. No, she couldn't believe that he would falter.

Are you ready?

You can never have too much preparation, she thought as she went over the details for the hundredth time. Nothing was to be written, so she had to rely on her memory. There wasn't much as far as she was concerned, she kept telling herself, but he had said many times that the smallest detail was as important as the biggest, and on each and every detail would depend the success or failure.

Now with only a short time to go, Kate tried to think of something else so that when the time came for total concentration, she would be able to give it full measure. She tried but was able to think of other things for only minutes at a time. Quickly her mind would return to the next few hours which might be, for her, Steve, and the others, disaster.

Time and again she saw in her mind's eye the turn of the cylindrical device that would signal his survival. But he had told her not to look because it might draw someone's attention to it. She thought it would take a superhuman effort on her part not to do so. She still did not know whether she could avert her eyes when the time came.

If everything were to end today, she would have no regrets. At least that was the way she hoped she would feel. But then again, there were so many things they could have done, so many good times they could have had together, and now she had the almost desperate urge to tell him that she loved him. *It can't end without Steve knowing how I feel about him, how much I love him. It must not end that way.* Not now that she was so sure of herself and in the truest knowledge of her love for Steve.

'Don't look at it,' he had told her. He would be there, he had said. And he had said it with the sweeping confidence of absolute and certain belief.

She had no thoughts for her own safety during those last few hours, no thoughts that she would do anything but what he had told her to do. All she wanted to do now was to tell him that she loved him. And she would, damn it!

Summoning all the conviction and confidence that he had given her, she was able to gain the level of unconditional resolve during those last few hours.

Why was she doing it? Because he had told her to? She thought not. To be rich? No, that didn't matter so much. To get back at financiers, bankers, big shots like Roy and the odious Monty? Probably not. And Steve, why was he doing it? To beat the system? To defeat those insurance people? Possibly. To do something, to be someone different. Did it matter now? No, it didn't matter. What mattered was her love for him and his for her. That's what mattered, and if she could fulfill her part and have it end so that they would be together, that's what mattered and nothing else.

Nor could she rationalize robbing the old lady as an act of love. it was not. But it wasn't an act of violence, either. With Steve she had a tremendous desire to give, and yet be taken, to yield uncompromisingly, yet retain. Again she asked herself again and again, 'Are you ready?'

'All right!' Steve said in a clear but now absolutely calm voice. 'Now get ready—five, four, three. Here we go! Two, one!'

Matt pushed down hard on the plunger of the firing box.

There was a colossal explosion from inside the tunnel. Dirt and dust blew out at them with the force of a small hurricane. They were so close that the stupefying noise from the blast almost deafened them. None, save Matt, knew how loud it would be.

In the great hall, it sounded like a cannon going off. Heads turned anxiously as a second boom was heard and then a third and then a fourth. But now the tellers, guards, and customers could see where the noise was coming from. A fat man dressed in a Santa Claus costume was beating thunderously on a big bass drum. He stood in about the center of the great hall and continued to beat boomingly until he was joined by several other Santas, forming a band. Trombone, trumpet, bassoon, and other instruments began playing one of the more spirited Christmas melodies. Their booming musical sounds filled the surrounding ground floor area and then ricocheted off and around the walls of the great bank's hall.

Customers and bank personnel were smiling now. The alarm that at first showed on their faces was replaced with smiles. A happy surprise, no doubt instituted by the usually staid bank. With one exception—Mr Bishop—everyone in the crowded great hall was delighted. He called to one of the assistants, 'Who authorized this?'

'I'm sure I don't know, sir. Certainly not me,' replied the young man, who along with most of the people in the bank, was enjoying the music.

'Well, get rid of them,' Bishop said tersely. 'I mean discretely. It is Christmas Eve.'

Immediately following the explosion, Steve, with Matt right behind him, crawled quickly to the end of the tunnel. They could see right away that Matt had done an expert job. A round chunk of concrete about two feet across had dropped out of the floor above as neatly as if it had been made that way, and it now rested on the floor of the tunnel. It gave them just enough clearance to climb into the hole left by the block Matt had extracted as neatly as a dentist would a tooth.

'Beautiful, Matt!' Steve exclaimed. 'Just beautiful!'

'I told you not to worry,' Matt said, a note of pride evident in his voice.

Steve inched his way up between the block and the roof until his head was in the gaping hole. With the aid of a flashlight, he could see the hole had been blasted all the way through to the crypt-like room. And the slab of concrete he stood on was actually part of the vault floor.

He couldn't see much, however, as the entrance they made was deep inside and furthest away from the larger area and the vault's steel door.

'All right', Steve called back along the tunnel, 'bring up the rest of the gear. We're in!'

A cheer might have broken out from those who were waiting in worried silence at the other end of the makeshift passageway, but they just sort of smiled at each other. Johnny and the others quickly made their way into the tunnel, each dragging a duffle bag. Mark and Johnny each made another trip to bring up the two remaining bags.

<hr />

There was a great deal of noise and commotion in the great hall as several more Santas appeared. Mr Bishop remonstrated with some of them as they passed. None of them paid him any heed as they were, by then, running around the bank ringing bells, banging drums, and, 'Ho, ho, hoing.'

And the band played on with gusto.

The revelries seemed to cause some disruption and confusion among bank employees, but they dealt with it in friendly fashion.

Mr Bishop gathered two of his aides and the bank guards, and together they tried to get rid of the Santa band and the other Santas. But the added difficulty was that many of the customers had blissfully joined in the merriment.

Steve was the first to climb into the vault and then Matt. The five duffle bags came next, handed up by the others. Then very quickly, the others, led by Luke, climbed in over Matt's rock.

Assembled, they waited for Steve to make sure they had brought all the remaining gear. The area in which they stood was walled with several heavy cabinets and other metal boxes set in rows and stacked almost to the ceiling.

It was eerily silent inside the vault; none of the clamour from the outside could be heard. There were no sounds, save Matt's laboured breathing in the tomb into which they had blasted their way.

Steve inspected the bags, making sure that everything was in order. Then with him leading the way, they went into the vault's main area. They moved through the arched entrance and into the larger area. Then they stopped and stood there staring, dumbfounded.

There were shelves running along both sides of the vault, one foot off the floor, with spaces between. They stood a little more than halfway to the ceiling. And on the shelves, money.

Before them was a low shelf upon which lay stack upon stack of currency. Neatly bound bundles of notes arranged in perfect order, each bundle tightly wrapped in a brown and blue band of paper.

Paralyzed, it seemed, into immobility at the sight, none of them seemed to be able to do anything but stare. The words then uttered by Matt were the only sound to break the odd silence:

'Holy shit, the mother lode!'

Steve was finally able to find a voice, though certainly not his own. 'All right, let's get with it. You all know what to do.'

Nobody moved.

'Come on! Let's go.'

This time they were jolted into action. And since this, as with all parts of the operation, had been rehearsed, they moved, it seemed, by rote. Each had his job to do and set about it. After a few minutes, they were back to more or less normal, as though every day of their lives had been spent surrounded by millions of dollars in cash, and what they were doing was a daily routine.

First, they changed their clothes, dumping the old coveralls into a heap in the center of the room. Johnny's assignment was to carry all the discarded garments into the room they first entered and throw them down the hole. The new outfits looked outrageously out of place in the surroundings, but the rehearsals had the desired effect, and nobody seemed to notice any self-consciousness. Hats and other apparel were placed carefully on the floor further along, near the third room of the vault, at the end of which stood the inside of the massive steel door.

Steve looked at a metal cabinet for a few seconds. It was about five feet high and ran six feet long. Steve opened first one door and then the other. He backed up to stare for a few seconds. Inside were packages of notes six inches high and stacked on top of each other. Each package was secured with paper binding that kept the money tightly held together. And there were eighty packages in the cabinet.

Without taking his eyes from the stacks, Steve called to them. 'Over here. Put all this in the sacks. This is what we take.'

The large duffle bags were turned inside out to add their bright shade to the already strange contrasts of colors. Steve's tongue seemed to him as dry as sand. He vainly and nervously licked his lips in the hope of a little moisture as he reached out to take the first stack of money.

Mark held one of the inside-out duffle bags open so that Steve could throw the stacks into it. Steve bent down and stretched his arms out to the first stack. Once he had his hands on it, he thought it was thick and heavier than it should be. He inched it very carefully towards him. Mark shook the big bag invitingly as Steve moved it towards the duffle bag but did not throw the stack in immediately. He was about to drop it in, they all heard it.

'Stop! Stop what you're doing!'

CHAPTER 23

Zero Hour Minus Four Hours, Thirty Seconds

'Stop what you're doing!'

Standing on one of the high writing tables in the center of the great banking hall, outfitted neatly and unadventurously in unmatched, brightly colored skirt and jacket, and capped with an eye-catching bonnet from which slyly poked shocks of flaming red curls, she shouted, 'Stop! Stop what you're doing and listen to me. Now! I'm here to tell you that you can stop right now.' She bellowed her message out loud and clear. 'At this season of the year, we can all start over with joy and plenty for everyone simply by …,'

At that exact instant, Steve dumped the stack of money into the bag held by Mark.

'… by forsaking this love of money!'

Steve dropped more stacks into a bag, this one held by a grinning Johnny.

'We must amend that which needs to be amended and correct that which needs correcting. And above all, we must share the prosperity. Oh, yes, and renounce …'

Another stack dropped into Matt's bag. Steve laughed out loud at the sight of the huge grin on the old man's face.

'… greed!'

Inside the bank, confusion, noise, and disruption reigned. The music from the band increased to a booming level, and the girl in the bonnet had to reach for an even higher level for her voice to be heard.

Cyrus Bishop his aides, and the two guards tried valiantly to restore order and decorum to his premises. 'Who the hell is she?' he shouted.

But the Santa band drowned out his plea as they passed by on one of their continuing marches around and around the bank, blaring out "Jingle Bells" and other Christmas favourites.

Steve dropped a stack of money onto the floor but quickly retrieved it.

And she went on, 'There is a better way.'

In quick succession, Steve tossed two stacks at a time now into the bag held by Johnny, and then the same into Matt's and Mark's bags.

The great bank hall was a madhouse as the Santa band increased the pitch and volume with every step. The woman on the table was demanding attention with her non-stop, sermon-like harangue. 'There is a better way to redistribute the wealth.'

The five bags were quickly filled. Steve closed them by pulling on the heavy drawstrings, which also contained a locking device to secure the openings.

While Steve and the others were filling the sacks, Luke was working in the third room. Matt, now free of his duties for the moment, joined him. 'Can you really open that thing, Luke?' he asked.

Luke had removed a metal plate from the inside of the vault door and was unscrewing parts of the now-exposed mechanism. 'There's nothing to it, Matt.'

Mark joined them. He, too, was finished with his assignment. He watched as Luke easily removed yet another piece of complicated insides of the huge steel door. Then, noticing the maker's name written on the back plate lying on the floor, Mark read aloud, 'Massey Remolds Safe and Vault.'

Luke adjusted another piece of the intricate part of the vault mechanism. 'Nothing to it. From this side, that is. You see, vaults are made to keep people from getting into, not from getting out of.'

Matt shook his head in admiration. 'Luke has the hands of a surgeon.'

'There, that's it.' Luke ran his eye over the innards of the door. 'It's done,' he said quietly as he attached a clamp with a handle on each side to the counter side of the big wheel. He gently turned it an inch or so, testing. The grips moved easily, and he stopped.

'Steve', he called. 'I can open it now.'

'Okay,' Steve replied. 'We're finished in here.'

The noise and confusion in the hall had reached its crescendo. Mr Bishop—tie askew, hair messed up, one side of his eyeglasses seemed to be bent out of shape—was still trying to restore order. But by that time, his physical condition was much weakened. The red-wigged woman continued her speech as the band of Santas began its last march around the bank.

Steve's watch read forty-nine hours and fifty-nine minutes into the operation as he looked at the faces of his partners. They stood facing him, still but alert, and ready.

Luke stood waiting for the command to open the great door. To Steve, looking at the upper part of their faces—that was all he could see as they had donned hats and the rest of the outfits—it seemed that with the only light coming from behind them, they took on an almost righteous appearance. 'Ready?' he asked.

'We're ready.' Matt answered for all of them.

'Okay, then. Zero minus twenty seconds!'

The Santas were near the far end of the bank, about to swing around and march past the great vault door for the last time.

'Stand by,' Steve said quietly. 'All right everyone, stand by. Seven, six, five, four, three.' They hoisted the sacks. 'Two, one!'

A loud buzzing sound emanated from Steve's watch.

'Go, Luke!' he yelled. 'Zero hour!'

161

If anyone inside the bank was looking, they would have seen the wheel turn very fast, and the great vault door open as the Santas marched past. They would have seen Steve and the others—now dressed in the same Santa costumes, hats, and beards and carrying the same red-velvet bags—emerge from the door to join the line of Santas. Steve and the others walked quickly and quietly out of the vault. Luke, the last man out, closed the door and spun the wheel.

But no one was looking.

The people in the bank were all too diverted with all the other things going on inside the great hall of the Montague Bank of Boston.

Each of the Santa marched all the way from one end of the bank to the other. But this time, went straight on out the front door.

Cyrus Bishop was in a state of near collapse. He had shouted and ranted until the bank was finally starting to clear. They were leaving, the Santa band and all the Santas, the crowds of customers and others who simply walked in to see what was going on. They were all leaving now.

Cyrus stood alone amid the litter of streamers and other seasonal paraphernalia in the great hall, the big vault door at his back. He no longer paid any heed to the woman still prattling on. He could still hear her, but it didn't matter anymore. His only motion was to remove a paper party hat that someone had placed on his head.

'What riches do we seek?' she cried. 'Fortune? No! Fame? No! It's the old values—honesty, honour, and love. Those are our riches!'

Then she let herself down smoothly from the table and walked out of the bank along with everyone else.

Kate congratulated herself on what must surely have been her best acting performance.

CHAPTER 24

Relax, It's Done

That night, several hours later, Kate walked slowly down the staircase of the old mansion dressed in a stunning, long evening dress. She looked regal in the way she descended, one unhurried step after another.

Steve and the others were in the drawing room, now greatly changed from the weary and dirty way they had emerged from the tunnels. They were neat and smartly attired in lounge suits and smart jackets. They were shaved, bathed, and most important, rested.

Not entirely rested, of course. Most of them thought they would sleep for a week after their recent activities. But after a few hours, they seemed ready to get back to a normal sleep pattern and had decided—Steve had given them the option—of going out for a drink and a good dinner.

There had been no trouble finding the van where Kate had parked it or separating themselves from the other Santas once they had left the bank. All the 'straight-pay' Santas dispersed quickly, mingling into the busy crowds of shoppers on Beacon Street.

Once in the van, they discarded the Santa outfits and beards, tossing them into plastic bags. They changed back into to the outfits they wore from the beginning of the long journey through the water tube, tunnels, and vault.

All heads turned towards Kate as she entered the drawing room. Those who were seated followed Matt's lead and stood. There was a reserved silence at first. Then Kate moved smoothly into Steve's arms.

The others crowded around. Kate felt obliged to hug everyone, which she did enthusiastically, from a 'daughterly' embrace for Matt, to the smack kisses on each of Luke's cheeks, causing, 'uh has' from the others.

Mark handed Kate a champagne glass. Steve filled it for her. 'Hmmm, thank you, Steve.' She waited before taking a sip as she could see he was was about to say something.

Steve sort of nodded them into a circle and smiled. The glasses were filled, but nobody drank, not yet. In rather formal silence they waited for Steve to speak.

'Lady and gentlemen', he said softly, 'congratulations. Let us take a drink on the success of our venture.'

They clicked each other's glasses. Matt bowed slightly to the others, and they drank as one.

None of them downed all the wine. Then they stood quietly until Kate broke the silence.

'Champagne, the drink for special occasions. I think I like it.'

'Me too,' the high-spirited Luke said. 'I've only tasted it once before, but I like it. I think it's all I'm going to drink from now on. If we run out, we can buy our own champagne company.'

'That would be a vineyard, Luke,' Matt murmured. 'Grapes. In this case, French grapes.'

'Oh, yeah, of course. A vineyard,' Luke agreed. 'A nice little vineyard.'

They were a contented group as they took seats and began to chat pleasantly about lighter stuff, of anything and of nothing. Just chit-chat, and there wasn't much of that really. It would be some time before they would want to talk about what they had done in any depth. More likely, it would be never.

Kate wanted to know what happened down there, but for now, she asked no questions.

The conversation died. The men were extremely tired. They wanted to relax and not put more strain on their used-up bodies than necessary.

Kate, looking over the rim of her glass, could see the weariness in them all, but mostly in Matt as he sat quietly in a large armchair. His hefty frame seemed to have sagged a good deal since she last saw him. Only the twinkle in his eye, a little dulled to be sure, told her his spirit, though perhaps a little damaged, was still high.

Johnny and Mark were okay but would need a few days to be fully fit again. Luke would laugh one minute and the next ready to fall asleep. Steve, she thought, had paced himself best for he knew what stresses would be placed on them and was, therefore, best able to control his physical and emotional outputs.

'Steve?' Kate said quietly.

'Yes, Kate.'

'May I take a look?'

'At?'

'It!' Kate said, prepared play.

Steve carefully placed his glass on the table. 'Sure', he said, standing. 'Come with me.'

He walked Kate towards a door leading off the room and furthest away from the hall entrance at the other end of the drawing room. Reaching the door, he paused. He turned to the others who still sat but had watched their movement across the room. 'Why don't we all take a look?'

They put down the glasses and joined Kate and Steve.

Assembled around the door, Steve waited for a few seconds and then opened it, leading them into the room. They stood still in the semi-darkness. Then Steve turned the light switch. And before them, the money.

It was neatly stacked, very much resembling the way it was inside the cabinet in the bank vault. Row upon row, stack upon stack. It hardly seemed possible, after all they had been through, that five men could carry such a load. In weight alone, it looked pretty staggering. Yet there it was, bundles of money tightly packed in binding tape.

No one tried to touch the money. They seemed content just to see it before them.

'How much is there, Steve?' Kate asked.

'The dollar count?'

'Yes.'

'Forty million.'

'How do you know how much it is?' Luke asked.

Steve didn't answer right away. Instead, he moved closer to the stacks, a tight smile on his face.

'I know.'

'Man, forty million,' Matt said softly. Even though it was barely a whisper, they all heard.

'I guess we could count it,' Luke said.

'We could do that, I suppose. But why? The bank will have an exact figure for us about a day after the discovery, which will be on Monday. Tomorrow is Christmas, that's Friday. Then Saturday and Sunday, the bank is normally closed anyway. Yes, they'll confirm the count by Tuesday, I think. But believe me, it's forty million.'

Mark could see something wrong in this reasoning. 'I've heard that people will overstate their losses in big robberies for insurance purposes. Isn't that right?'

'Overstate for some reason,' said Steve. 'I guess that happens, but in this case, I think we can confidently place our trust in the bank.'

Luke gulped. 'I still can't believe it. I believe it when I see it, but when it's out of my sight, I can't believe it.'

They stood chatting and looking at the money for a few more moments. Then they looked at each other. It seemed there was nothing more to say.

Johnny broke the awkward silence, first with a soft cough. Then he asked, 'So, what now?'

Steve felt this might be leading to an unwanted moment. 'Okay', he announced, 'a fine dinner, a *really* fine dinner. I made reservations weeks ago, so let's not be late.'

'Right', said Luke. 'I'll just run upstairs and get my coat.'

'Don't be long, Luke,' Steve told him.

'Back in a minute. Want me to get yours, Matt?'

'Mine's in the hall, Luke.'

'Okay.'

Luke raced up stairs like the boy he really was, not trying to conserve his remaining energy one bit. He entered the high-ceilinged bedroom with the big bay window and grabbed the coat. He was about to run back down the stairs when he noticed the plastic bag lying on the floor near the bed, where he had dropped it earlier.

Each man had been responsible for bringing his outfit with him from the van. On a whim, he donned the Santa hat and stood for a second before the full-length mirror situated by the bay window. Then he sprinted downstairs and back to the others.

'Ho-ho-ho!' he murmured in a low tone and the best Santa voice he could muster as he thumped into the drawing room.

'Cut the clowning, Luke,' Mark said. 'We've got some celebrating to do.'

Luke quickly removed the hat and got his coat from where he had left it on the banister with a last, 'Ho-ho-ho!'

'And this is the kid who opened that great big, old vault,' Johnny mused, shaking his head.

'You bet he did,' Matt said smiling broadly.

◆━━━·······━━◆━━━·······━━◆

While Luke was putting on the Santa hat, a car drove by the old mansion, passing just across the street from the big bay window before which Luke had stood at the mirror with his back to the window.

The occupants were a man, his wife, and in the back seat, a little girl. The moment the car was abreast of the old mansion, the child just happened to look up at the window and saw Luke. 'Daddy, Daddy, stop!' the little girl shouted. 'Mommy, it's Santa Claus. Look, he's up there!'

The man and his wife, travel weary from a long trip, were not about to indulge their child and paid little attention to her. And if they had done so, Luke had already left the room, and the light had gone out.

'Daddy, Daddy!' the little girl cried excitedly.

'That will do, Kathy. We're almost home,' her mother said a little impatiently.

'I saw him,' Kathy insisted irritably. 'Santa!'

'Enough, Kathy,' the man said. 'Look, we're at the driveway.'

'But, Mommy', cried the little girl, 'I really did see Santa.'

Tears of exasperation were about to overflow down her cheeks. The car turned into the driveway and pulled to a stop at the front door.

Mark and Johnny checked windows and door latches through the house. Then leaving the light burning in the drawing room, they all moved out through the hall to the car parked in the circular driveway.

In another driveway two houses away, the couple unloaded their car. 'Here, Kathy,' her dad said, handing a toy behind him as he leaned into the car. 'You can take some of your own things, Kathy. Kathy!'

'She went inside already.'

<hr />

'Where are we going, Steve?'

'An excellent restaurant, Kate. It has a small nightspot if your not too tired. Not a big night, though.' Steve drove, with Kate sitting between him and Mark. The other three were in the back seat, Luke in the middle.

Steve started the car and eased it gently down the driveway, slowing to a halt before turning into the street. Inside the car, they chatted quietly. As the car glided out of the driveway, they did not see Kathy's tiny figure at the gate of the house next door, Raggedy Anne doll in hand.

CHAPTER 25

Kathy and Raggedy Anne

'I'm telling you, dam it, that I've looked everywhere,' the hysterical mother yelled at her husband. 'She's not in the house! Can't you get that through your head, for Christ's sake?'

'Now don't get excited, Louise.'

'I am excited. And you would be, too, if you had any goddam brains.'

'Louise!'

'Oh, shut up! Did you look out front?

'Yes, and the street.'

'I think I should check. Maybe she's—'

'Call the police!' Kathy's father shouted.

'Now wait.'

'Call the police, dammit!'

'I'm going to look in the backyard again. Maybe she ...'

'Call the police! Kathy's father shouted again. 'If you don't, I will!'

Louise picked up the receiver and pressed the keys. 'Asshole!'

Kathy had safely waited for the car to go past her. Then she walked up the driveway towards the big house and knocked on the door. Receiving no answer, she went around to the back. She knocked on the back door and got the same result. But she was determined to see Santa. So she returned to the front door and tried to push it open. When she couldn't, she began knocking on the door again, harder and louder this time.

<hr />

'Champagne, I guess,' Matt said to the hovering waiter. 'The Dom Pérignon. I assume that's the best you have.'

Steve had only a passing knowledge of wines and all matters culinary, for that matter, so he deferred to Matt as a gesture. And Matt, after ignoring the wine list, had given the order.

But Mark had other ideas. 'Just a second, Matt. I believe I owe Johnny a beer.' He glanced over to the other side of the table. 'Right, Johnny?'

'Absolutely. Corona.'

Mark nodded. 'I think I'll join you. Corona beer for me.'

Matt chimed in, 'In that case, beer for me also.'

'No champagne?' Luke asked, disappointed.

'Have whatever you want, Luke,' Steve said. 'But I guess I'm for a beer as well. Kate?'

'Sure. We had the traditional thing, so beer all round!'

'Okay', Luke agreed and laughed.

The famous old restaurant Steve had selected long before the enterprise began was The Cafe Royal, and it was fashioned after the one in London of the same name. Plush red velvet seating in large booths and tables under glittering chandeliers, the place was an anachronism of another not so recently past century, comfortable and rich for the rich and comfortable.

Steve had chosen a booth towards the rear with a good view of the rest of the classy establishment. It was close to the band, but not so close as to be disturbed by the music, which was just the right kind of melodies that generated a pleasant ambiance.

'But for the food, Steve,' Matt said, 'I think I'll ask you to do the ordering.'

'Already taken care of, Matt. I hope you all approve of my selections. Let's see, I asked them to have the duck l'orange available. It's a specialty here, among others. There's a really fine list, from duck to English roast beef. But, of course, you will want to make your own choices. Whatever you select, it's all first rate.'

'I'm sure it is,' Kate said. 'Steve, let's dance.'

'Sure.' Steve took her hand.

'Oh, no. You're tired. Forget it.'

'It's okay. But just once around the block, okay?'

'Okay.'

The others remained seated as Steve and Kate walked over to the small square in front of the bandstand, where several other couples were dancing. They moved easily together to the music of a slow dance tune.

⁕

'They're sending someone around,' Louise said agitatedly. 'They didn't say how long it would take for them to get here. Shit! There's never a cop around when you need one.'

'Louise, please watch your language when they get here.'

'Oh, go fuck yourself!'

'Please.'

'Don't you get it? Our daughter's missing!'

⁕

Kathy could find no entrance at either front or rear, so she began to investigate other means of entry. All the windows she could reach were locked securely, as were the small basement ones.

But as all persistence is rewarded in some fashion, Kathy finally found an open latch on a small basement window. After several unsuccessful attempts, she was eventually able to pry it a little with her tiny fingers and then push it completely open. She made her way up the stairs of the old house. Kathy was totally fearless in her quest for the elusive Santa Claus.

⁂

Steve and the others were enjoying the promised excellent dinner. Luke had wanted to order the duck, but Matt advised against it, saying it was too rich for a stomach that had been, over the last three days, exposed only to basic though nutritious food and was not ready to accept such highly seasoned victuals. Luke eventually agreed and settled on a veal specialty.

Matt, notwithstanding the good advice to his younger companion, did away manfully with two large portions of the roast beef and Yorkshire pudding, while the others had a variety of fine dishes. They deferred to the waiter's suggestion for dessert, however, of trifle supreme, served with great globs of fresh cream whipped to a delicious stiffness. The men had coffee and cognac, while Kate sipped on a crème de la cacao.

Enjoying the last part of the sumptuous spread, they talked quietly about many subjects, savoring the leisurely pace of the surroundings. As their table was set in an alcove almost at the rear of the restaurant, diners at nearby tables could not overhear their conversation. Mark, therefore, felt safe in making the first reference to the exploit.

'Steve?' he said.

'Yes, Mark.'

'I want to ask you something.'

'Fire away.'

'How did we pull it off?'

'Time and motion.'

'As simple as that?' Johnny chipped in.

Steve shook his head. 'None of it was simple. It was timed to exactitude, and the motion—that is, all of us—were organized to every specific task so as to match up precisely with that timing.'

Two of them started to ask something. 'Just a second. Let me finish. The fact is that you can't alter time, of course, but you can alter the events that take place in that time. And that is what we did.'

'Okay then, how could it happen?' Mark asked. 'I mean, how could we have done it? Oh, I know it's done and all, but well, I don't know how to phrase my question, but …'

'I think I know what you're saying. Why wasn't it preventable?'

'Well, yes,'

'Okay.' Steve took a deep breath. 'You see, the police and other security agencies will freely admit that it is impossible to prevent most crime. They can only hope, at best, to catch the perpetrators after a crime has been committed. Then put the criminals away, thereby eliminating the possibility of those criminals at least committing other crimes. While they are incarcerated, that is. Also, this kind of crime detection is one of the lower, less absolute sciences. Not like say, murder. Those sciences are very advanced stuff, like DNA and that kind of thing. Now, take our recent experience, okay?'

'Okay', said Matt on behalf of all of them.

'We approached our multiple and varied problems with the mission in the most scientific way possible. Every detail was worked out in advance. Every piece of equipment was made especially for the specific part of the operation for which it was intended; each piece of clothing was made to order for the individual who would wear it. Imagine a simple thing like say blistered feet. If the boots we wore didn't fit, where would our timing be if we were held up by just one member of the group? Don't you agree?'

'Yes, but—' Mark had other questions.

'No, wait a minute, Mark,' Steve interrupted. 'Let me finish.'

'Okay.'

'I worked on details so minute that most reasonable people could easily discount them as improbabilities. But it was necessary to eliminate any possible chance of failure. If the world's most efficient police departments and crime prevention agencies, from the FBI to Scotland Yard and the French Sêreté, agree that you cannot prevent a crime from being committed, if the perpetrators of that crime are totally committed and determined to do so, then you are left with only one other option.'

Again he paused to look around the table, noting that he had their full attention. 'Then if we agree that crime prevention is not a science, we have *made*', he emphasized the word *made*, 'a science out of this particular operation. That's right, a complete science, science being a knowledge of facts, phenomena, and proximate causes gained and verified by exact observation, experiment, and analysis. So by the time we had all the information we needed, what we did was surely only the mechanics of the operation. That's all.'

'And,' Matt said, 'the determination to do it.'

'That, too, yes.'

'A determined man,' Matt said, touching his forehead with the tips of his fingers as though seeking clarity. 'Yes, that's it. A determined man once set to his task cannot be denied.'

'I got this one! Herodotus, right?' Luke almost shouted.

'No.'

'Euripides?'

'Nope.'

'Who then?'

'Me.'

'You? You're a smart old geezer, Matt.'

'Old, yes. Geezer? Perhaps.' He smiled.

There was a long moment when no one said anything, digesting what Steve had explained. It made sense, and he had made it very clear to them. And anyway, the fact remained that they had achieved, under Steve's direction, what they had set out to do.

'You mentioned one other option,' Johnny said.

'I'm coming to that,' said Steve. 'So if crime prevention doesn't work, the authorities are left with the other option on which to concentrate their efforts—crime detection. Now then, if a perpetrator has been thorough and precise, he is going to leave very little for investigators to work with. Let's see, some coveralls made out of cloth that is sold in stores by the millions of yards each year, gas, oxygen acetylene bottles, hoses, and torches available anywhere. Some wheeled trucks and a harpoon gun could have been made by anyone, not necessarily an engineer like Mark.'

Steve paused for a moment to look at his friends again then went on.

'No, gentlemen and Kate, the list of what authorities do not have to work with could go one much longer. But the list of what they do have is much shorter. They'll probably round up a few known criminals, try to pry information out of informants, and issue, from time to time, unabashed statements about important new developments and other such face-saving boloney.'

He looked directly at Mark as he concluded with the observation, 'I hope that answers your questions.'

Mark nodded. 'It does.'

'I have a question.'

'Ask away, Johnny.'

'Okay, here it is. How do you convince people to do what you want? I mean you.'

Steve rubbed his chin and thought about it for a moment. 'Well, there are a great many words that can inspire others to act on them. Stringing certain words together to get an effect is one way. You just have to make people feel what you have said is exactly what they were thinking and what they wanted to do. Simple really.'

'Hmm, okay, I guess.'

'Good.' He smiled. 'You see', Steve placed his hands palm up on the white tablecloth and shrugged for emphasis. 'Once the people were doing what you expected they would do, and the organization of all of parts was in place, all we had to do was do it.' He smiled broadly. 'There was nothing that could go wrong!'

<hr />

'Okay, let's see if I've got it,' the formidable police sergeant said. 'She's five years old, blue eyes, blonde hair. She's very bright, and she's not afraid of the dark. Right?'

'Or of anything!'

'Okay, ma'am. You said she was willful and hard to control. Ah, your words, not mine.'

'Come on now, Louise. Most of the time she's like not that. And besides—'

'Shut up!' she interrupted. 'Shut the hell up!'

Kathy had found the stairs leading up from the basement to the kitchen of the big house. Although mostly dark, some moonlight came from the windows near the ground level of the basement, and on reaching the upper area, the darkness was not so dense, she could see fairly well. She went through the kitchen and into the back hallway, making her way towards the drawing room. The lights were on in the drawing room, and like a moth, she was attracted to them. She moved slowly, all the while holding tightly to Raggedy Anne.

Kathy stood in the archway of the drawing room and looked around. Then in the tiniest of voices, she called, 'Santa?'

She moved almost to the center of the room and was about to turn and run to the stairs, thinking Santa might still be where she saw him from the car. As she turned, Kathy saw it. Lying there on a lounge chair, where Luke had tossed it, was the Santa Claus hat. The little girl grabbed it. Her confidence boosted, she bellowed, 'Santa, I know you're here. Where are you, Santa?'

Her lively little mind figured that if she saw Santa upstairs and now here was his hat, he was probably down the ground floor. So she began to look around. Almost immediately she saw a door leading off the drawing room, away from the archway through which she had entered. Kathy headed straight for it.

***

The crackle of the police radio in the patrol car cut through the crisp winter air in the otherwise silent tree-lined street. The sergeant left the house after trying to calm the hysterical mother, achieving as much success as did her husband.

'Boy', he said. 'Did she have a mouth on her or what? And them rich as hell too.'

Another black and white pulled behind the sergeant's car, in which another officer sat listening for reports. Two more policemen were accompanied by a female officer in a second car. In the intermittent glare of the rotating roof beacons, the sergeant gathered the others around him and gave them the details and description of the quarry.

'All right, now. You've got the description of the kid. We'll canvass the houses on this street and the immediate vicinity. Her name is Kathy. Let's go!'

Kathy wrestled with the big, old-fashioned doorknob. She finally had to put her Raggedy Anne doll on the floor so she could use both hands. Then it turned for her. Soon she would be face-to-face with Santa. She picked up the doll, pushed open the door, and went inside.

'Sorry to disturb you, sir. We're looking for a lost child.' The police officer made the inquiry several houses from the old mansion, but other officers were heading in that direction.

CHAPTER 26

What Could Go Wrong?

The car was brought to the front of the restaurant. The attentive head waiter and the hatcheck girl helped Steve and the others with their coats.

Steve's tip, on the American Express card with which he had paid the bill was a more than adequate, but not ostentatiously so. The man would have been just as gracious regardless of the amount. He was a professional on all counts. Steve chatted with him pleasantly. 'My compliments, maître 'd,' Steve said. 'Excellent.'

'Merci, monsieur. It was a pleasure.'

And then they were on their way home.

'Sorry to bother you, ma'am, but we're looking for a little girl, lost.'

Kathy walked into the room. In the light cast from the drawing room, she could see a lot of shelves with stacks of things on them. She moved slowly beside the rows of bank notes. She glided her tiny hand over them, lightly touching the ones she could reach. Kathy knew what money was, but it was the overall prettiness that really attracted her as she moved from one end of the shelf to the other.

Then she thought she heard someone, not her mother, calling, 'Kathy', but she was not listening much anyway. She picked up one of the bundles of money and held it against Raggedy Anne.

'Kathy! Kathy!'

This time she heard it plainly. Someone was calling her. The little girl began to run out of the room.

'Kathy!'

The voice was that of the policewoman walking up the driveway of the old mansion. Kathy was almost to the door leading back into the drawing room when she tripped and fell. Raggedy Anne and the bundle of bills went skittering away from her. Picking herself up, she looked for the two dropped items. The bundle of money had gone through the door and into the drawing room. It was lying half-hidden under a lounge chair, while the doll was in plain view.

Kathy!'

The voice was closer. She shouted, 'I'm here! I'm here in Santa's house.'

Police officer Joanne Nielson approached the front door of the old house. There seemed to be only one lighted room, and she hoped she would not have to disturb too many residents.

'Kathy!' she called again.

Kathy ran through the drawing room to the hallway. She had retrieved Raggedy Anne but not the package. She raced towards the voice as fast as she could. Her mother would be very angry.

'I'm here,' she shouted back as she wrenched hard on the old brass lock. Kathy pulled the front door open just as the policewoman was about to knock.

The warmth inside the car didn't help. They were feeling very tired and having a hard time keeping their eyes open. Steve blinked sleepily.

'Want me to drive?' Kate asked as she snuggled up to him.

'No, I'm okay, thanks. And it's not far. No traffic now either. We'll be there before you know it.'

'You're okay now, Kathy,' the policewoman said as she took hold of the little girl's hand. 'Your mommy and dad are very worried.'

'This is Santa's house,' announced the smiling five-year-old.

'We'll have you back home soon.'

'Come look at all the presents.'

'Just a minute, Kathy. Now let's just stand there for a minute.' The officer spoke into a walkie-talkie. 'Nielson here. I found the little girl, 216 North Beaumont. She's okay.'

Kathy struggled to get loose from policewoman's grip, but the best she could manage was to pull the woman by the hand into the hallway and towards the drawing room.

'Okay, okay! Kathy, listen to me. Is there anyone else here?'

'Come on, I'll show you.'

'Did someone bring you here, Kathy?'

'Look, I'll show you,' Kathy said, pulling the policewoman.

'Hello', the police sergeant yelled as he walked up to the front door.

'In here, Sergeant.'

The other policemen were coming up the driveway.

'Is there anyone else here?' the sergeant asked.

'Apparently not,' she told him. 'Looks like she just wondered in. Door must have been wide open.'

'Yeah, I guess. Hello, Kathy. Listen, did someone bring you here, honey?' the sergeant asked.

'No. I saw Santa.'

'Sure, but did Santa bring you in here. You know the folks who live here?'

'Uh, uh, no.'

'Well, she seems okay. Go tell the parents. Smithy, take a look around. See if there's anyone home.'

The sergeant moved into the drawing room followed by Harrison, but with a tight hold on the little girl's hand. She seemed to want to drag him towards another room.

'Get the kid back to her folks.'

'Okay.'

At that moment, Steve's car turned into the driveway. He could see that the front door was open. When they were about halfway up the tree-lined drive, a patrol car with lights flashing roared up the driveway right behind him.

'Steve, what's happening?' Kate asked in a stunned whisper.

'I don't know.'

The others began to stir.

'Okay, just hold on, till we—'

'What the hell?' Someone in the back said.

'Sit tight,' Steve said.

He pulled the car to a stop at the front entrance. A cop was standing at the door. 'What's up officer?' Steve called without getting out of the car. He could see other police vehicles coming round the driveway circle behind him. He left the engine running.

'You live here?'

'Well, yes, what is—'

'Little girl got lost, maybe got herself into this place. I guess they're searching now. You better come in. The sergeant's inside with a bunch of other cops.'

'Search, they're searching?' Steve asked. The excellent repast was boiling up to nausea in his stomach as he got out of the car. The others followed. They entered the house and went into the drawing room.

Five police officers were more or less wandering around. A policewoman was holding the hand of a little girl. She, along with the other cops, looked at Steve suspiciously.

Behind her, Steve could see that the door leading off from the drawing room was standing more than halfway open.

'The sergeant', Steve asked, 'They said he's here.' He didn't wait for her to answer instead shouted in a panicky voice, 'Sergeant!' And at the same time, he stated walking quickly towards the open door.

'Sergeant!' he called louder this time.

'Okay, okay. Hold it down.' The sergeant stood behind a high-backed winged chair facing the open door.

Steve had rushed right by without seeing him. He now turned to see the sergeant using the back of the high-backed chair as support for his notebook.

He gave Steve a cursory glance. 'You the owner?'

'I, I rent it,' Steve said.

'Okay. Same thing.'

Kathy's mother rushed into the room and grabbed the little girl. 'Kathy, Kathy. Thank God you're all right.'

'I wanted to see Santa.'

'We're going home,' she said and hurried out of the room, holding Kathy tightly.

She was followed by her husband, who turned to the cops. 'Gee, officers. We're sorry, ah, very sorry. I mean—'

But his wife's shrill voice cut off whatever else he was about to say. 'Oh, come on, you useless asshole!'

The moment he walked into the room, Matt saw the money bundle sticking out from under one of the chairs. He wandered over slowly, past the sergeant and Steve, and sat down heavily, kicking the bundle all the way under the chair with the heel of his shoe. The sergeant looked at Matt curiously for a moment, and then turned a less-than-friendly grimace on Steve.

'Looks like a lot of valuable stuff here.'

'I don't understand,' Steve replied.

'Oh, really?' The rather irritated police sergeant exhaled heavily to demonstrate his exasperation. 'Jesus, haven't you heard of, oh, I don't know, like burglars?'

Steve looked at him and said nothing.

'Look,' the sergeant motioned around the room with his free hand, 'we do our best to prevent crime, right? And you people leave a joint like this open so even a little kid can get in. Jesus!'

Steve looked as though he was beginning to regain his composure.

The sergeant moved away from the chair and came towards Steve, who stood between him and the door to the money room.

When he got close enough, Steve took his arm and adroitly turned him around the other way, at the same time closing the door.

'That was stupid of me, Sergeant. Christmas celebrations and all, you understand.' Steve walked him towards the front door. 'Sorry for the trouble, Sergeant. I apologize. And of course, Merry Christmas.'

'Well, yeah, Merry Christmas. Merry Christmas all.' The sergeant eased up a little, taking note of Kate and the others as though for the first time.

'While I'm here, maybe we should take a look around,' he said. He turned and started towards the door of the room where the money was. 'You know, to check with you if anything's missing.'

Steve quickly stepped in front of him. 'That's okay, Sergeant. It was just a little girl after all. Don't worry. It's fine, thanks,' he replied graciously, while at the same time, backing towards the front doorway more or less as an inducement for the cop to follow. 'Sorry again for any trouble.'

The police sergeant followed Steve's lead and was about to leave. Then he stopped and wheeled around on Steve and the others. 'Well,' he hesitated, looked at them, and then went on, 'okay then. Just be more careful. Lock up real secure all the stuff you got here. Do you get it? You folks gotta be more careful.'

'You're right, Sergeant,' Steve agreed. 'You are so right.'

CHAPTER 27

Merry Christmas

Everyone was in the drawing room following a catered lunch Steve arranged, drinking coffee and relaxing. Everyone was rested and looked it.

'Now gentlemen,' Steve said, 'and Kate.'

'Thank you,' she said.

'Now then, we must decide what to do with the money. We agreed that there would be no division or spending of our proceeds until at least one year has passed.'

'A whole year,' Luke said and sighed.

'That's what we agreed, Luke,' Matt was quick to interject. 'We all said so.'

'That's right,' Mark agreed. 'Safer that way.'

'Yeah,' Johnny said, nodding. 'Sure.'

'Oh, of course,' Luke felt obliged to say. 'I only meant, well, nothing. Sorry.'

'Think of it this way, Luke. About a year from now, you'll have one hell of a New Year's Day to celebrate.' Steve said and smiled.

'Naturally, for the immediate future,' Steve went on, 'you will continue to live as close to normal, your jobs, where you reside, and so on. All that was also agreed, until such time as it is considered safe.'

There were more nods of approval.

'Since last night's lucky escape,' Steve began as he stood and walk around, 'well, I've been giving some thought to our little problem of where to put the money. I have some ideas, but I would like to hear any suggestions you might have.' He looked them over and took a seat. 'How about you, Mark?'

'A bank.' He laughed. 'Why not put it in a big bank's safe deposit boxes?'

'There's too much,' Steve responded. 'Too much bulk, I mean. It would mean splitting it up. And besides, where? Which one? I thought of that Mark, but there are too many things against it. Any other suggestions?'

'Can't think of anything.'

'Kate?'

'Why not rent an old house like this one. We could take turns at watching it. Someplace in the country or a small town, maybe?'

'Hmm, well yes. But the thing is, local people get suspicious of new residents,' Steve countered. 'Besides, there is so much that it would take only a workman, the mailman, a county employee, someone to get an idea and contact the authorities. We could also get robbed. There are all kinds of unexpected things that could happen. Also, don't forget last night. Johnny?'

'You got me. I think Kate's idea is the best, but you just shot the hell out of that.'

'That's the best I can come up with,' Kate said.

'Matt, how about you? What do you say?'

Matt who had sat quietly, listening throughout, a cup and saucer balanced delicately in his gnarled hands. 'For me,' he said, 'I guess my mind is already made up.'

'Where?' asked Kate.

'Okay, where, Matt?' Mark said.

Matt carefully placed the cup down on a small table before answering. 'Just wherever and however Steve has already decided. You see, I am perfectly content with the way Steve has steered the whole affair thus far, and I am confident his suggestion of where to hide the money for a year will be a good one. Also, I might add, my curiosity in respect to the actual location is not greatly roused.'

The answer was simple: Steve would handle it. And Matt had just articulated what all of them perhaps really thought.

'Thanks, Matt,' Steve said.

'Suits me too.'

'Sure,' Mark agreed.

'Okay by me,' Johnny went along.

'Fine,' Kate said, moving over to sit on the floor beside Steve's chair. 'But where?' Then, knowing him as well as she did, Kate added, 'You have it planned already, don't you?'

'Not quite. Let me work out a few details. I think I might have the perfect place.'

CHAPTER 28

New York

They made the return journey to New York City uneventfully, each using the same mode of transport as before, except for Steve. He used a rental van to make the trip. In the back were the boxes that had contained equipment for the job; they were now used to hold the money. Everyone had been busy since the meeting, removing the paper bands that held the bundles of bills together and burning the wrappers in the large fireplace. The money was placed in plastic trash bags, and those were placed in the boxes.

The wind whistled through the area where Steve, Mark, and Johnny worked. It was cold, damp, and dark. Very dark.

'Okay, first we have to move this stuff closer,' Steve said. 'Mark, put that over to the wall.'

'Over here?' Johnny wanted to be sure.

'That's it. Right.'

'Okay.'

Mark, who seemed to be able to maneuver better in the blackness than Steve, he easily lugged the large pieces away and returned. Johnny, like Mark, seemed to have little trouble moving around in the darkness.

'Okay, we can put them in now.' They lowered the bags in. 'We just place those slabs on top, and we're done.'

When they were finished, Steve checked his wristwatch. 'Four fifteen. Good.'

CHAPTER 29

Sun and Surf in the Bahamas

The next day they went to the Bahamas, all of them. Steve had made the arrangements several weeks before, long before he was even sure the deal was to made at all. It was a gamble he was prepared to take. He made the reservations at different times and made payments by a variety of methods. Some of the bookings had been made through travel agencies, others directly with the hotels.

Each left at different times on different airlines. Steve and Kate, however, had gone off together as a couple. He made sure there was nothing that could connect them to each other as a group. How they travelled was only one of the many ways he used from the very beginning.

Matt and Luke, although arriving on different airlines and times, were checked into the Elbow Beach Resort Hotel. Mark and Johnny went to the Coral Beach Hotel, both on the magnificent beachfront. All four occupied single rooms. Kate and Steve were at the less-elegant but still within the first-class range of hotels, the Blue Horizons Guest House, also facing the superb surf and sandy beaches.

Steve had, as he had in all the planning, been meticulously careful and left nothing to chance. Now that the money was secure, he felt comfortable and sure nothing could go wrong.

Steve and Kate enjoyed doing the usual things that were available in the attractive Bahamian resort. They swam in the warm Caribbean waters and ate lunch at one of the many beach cafes. At night they dined and danced in the sumptuous Eagles Nest restaurant on the top floor of the hotel or at one of the other nightspots. They relaxed—and waited for news from Boston to appear in the newspapers that Steve picked up every morning in the hotel lobby.

As people do on such holiday occasions, they all met casually in a cafe in front of one of the other resorts on the beach on the third day of their stay. They chatted and joked. There was no mention of the recent event that had brought them so close to each other. And that had more than once brought them close to disaster. Now they were safe, reinvigorated, and rested.

Every day Steve expected to read the news of the robbery in Boston. But there was nothing. By day 4 Steve anticipated the news of the robbery had to break, along with all the details police could give reporters. And that more details would emerge in the days that followed as the investigation continued. But there was nothing.

Perhaps the police were keeping it quiet for some reason. The robbery had to have been discovered after the holiday break. Steve was a loss to know what happened. He called the others to a meeting at another beach cafe on the fifth day. No one had any idea as to what must be going on back there in Boston.

'What do you think, Steve?' Matt asked him.

Steve shook his head and placed his hands face up indicating perplexity. 'I haven't got a clue.'

'Oh, Mr Rupert.'

Rupert Montague and Cyrus Bishop stood there staring at the great hole in the floor of the vault. Then Montague turned to look at where his money once lay securely in the steel cabinet, now empty.

'What I mean is what shall we do?'

Mr Montague didn't answer. He just stood there staring, transfixed on the empty cabinet.

'Mr Rupert. Mr Rupert!'

Finally Montague seemed to come back to himself. 'Who else has seen this?'

'Only us. Mr Simpson came to get me as soon as he opened the vault. That's right, isn't it, Simpson?' he said, turning to the chief cashier, standing at the door with an even whiter face than Bishop's.

'Yes, sir. I ran straight to your office. Oh, this is terrible! I'm so, Mr Montague, I don't know what to say. I … I …'

Montague could see that the man was beginning to babble. 'Calm yourself, Mr Simpson,' he said sharply.

There followed a few moments where no one said anything.

Rupert Montague turned to the vault entrance, where two guards were standing in the their usual positions, one on each side of the great vault door that now stood half open. If they were to look inside the vault, the guards would not be able to see the hole in the floor. To see it, they would have to be where Montague and the other two were standing.

Rupert Brady Montague seemed to come to a decision. He turned sharply to the other two. 'Mr Simpson.'

'Yes, sir?'

'Mr Simpson, I want you to go to your office, and stay there until I call you. All right?'

'Yes, sir, right away.'

He started to leave, but Montague stopped him. 'You are to say nothing about this to anyone. Is that quite clear?'

'Yes, sir.'

'Nothing. Do you understand?'

'Yes, nothing to anyone.'

'Thank you, Mr Simpson.'

He left, and Montague turned to Cyrus Bishop. 'Some things will have to be done. First—'

'Yes, of course,' Bishop interrupted. 'Call the police.'

'No.'

'But, but the money. We have to—'

'Mr Bishop!' he interrupted loudly. But he stopped and restarted almost immediately in a softer tone. 'Mr Bishop, I want this to stay between us.'

'But, but ...'

'Listen to me.' He took a breath. 'This is what I want you to do.' Another breath, deeper this time. 'First, I want you to instruct Simpson to move everything here to the other vaults and safes. Second,' he pointed to the hole in the vault floor, 'this is to be fixed. I want it to look as it did. I want concrete poured down that hole. I don't care if it takes a thousand tons of concrete, fill it, and replace the floor as it was.'

'Very well, but I don't see why we—'

'Mr Bishop!' His voice rose then stopped and again turned abruptly to a quiet, virtually indulgent tone. And for the first time in his life, he placed his hand on Bishop's shoulder and leaned in very close. 'Mr Bishop, Cyrus, this affair is to stay between us in total, *in total*. Is that absolutely clear?'

Cyrus Bishop looked at the man he had known all his professional life. 'Yes, if that's what you want. Yes, sir,' he said somberly.

'Thank you, Cyrus.'

And for a few minutes, they stayed like that. Not moving, not speaking. When Rupert Montague spoke again, his voice was soft, perhaps even philosophical.

This had changed everything. And yet, he seemed as though he was accepting of what? Of what had at first shocked him. Now it was a fact. The money, his money, was gone. His plans had dissolved in a fleeting moment. There would be no getaway. No European playboy life. No Swiss chalets. No French Riviera.

Rupert Brady Montague had made his decisions in almost that same span of time. He would restart his life with Carlota. They could—they would–be happy.

He turned from contemplations and decisions and faced Mr Bishop again. 'Cyrus, those things that you wanted to do, those things that I know I have resisted, your plans for expansion, yes, I know you have already started some of them. And, of course, they are good for the bank. You have done well.'

He stopped, but Bishop knew there was more.

'I want you to take on more responsibilities. As for myself, I'm going to spend more time with the family. Yes, that's what I'm going to do, time with my family. Cyrus,' he stopped abruptly and then took on an even more benign manner and tone of voice, 'Cyrus, I want you to take over the bank.'

Cyrus Bishop had waited a lifetime for a moment like this. A moment that he thought would never come. Inside he was staggered, but outwardly, it was his nature to appear calm.

'Thank you, Rupert.'

As Steve had planned, they stayed in the Bahamas for the full fourteen days. Two weeks, and still no news about the robbery. Steve was completely baffled. All that time spent planning and evaluating and calculating—What if this happened?—What if that happened? There was no doubt in his mind that he covered every possibility, every possible event. And now this. He could not fathom what happened. He wracked his brains time and time again and came up with nothing.

They returned to New York.

CHAPTER 30

Surprise!

Again they all went by separate means of transport, different airlines at different times. Steve would stick to the plan.

Kate and Steve arrived at Kennedy Airport late in the evening. They went on to the Sixty-First Street apartment, arriving just after eleven.

For no reason at all, Steve had a feeling. Late though it was, Steve went straight to where he and Mark and Johnny had parked the money. He knew he would find nothing to answer the question of why there was no news of the robbery. But he went there anyway because he couldn't think of anything else to do. And then again, there was that feeling.

So he got the team together. And he and Matt, Luke, Johnny, and Mark trooped to the building site in lower Manhattan. To the place where they met at the beginning of the whole operation, heading to the basement, where they had gotten together to confirm the pact they made.

Before it all began, Steve had gone over it a hundred or more times, trying to find things that could go wrong. He had gone back and checked everything time and again. There was nothing, nothing that could go wrong. Nothing.

Looking at the building now, he realized there was something that he had considered but dismissed.

There it was. The construction crews had restarted the building of the office block. Now the rickety fence on the sidewalk that had been so easy to walk right on thorough was a more substantial barrier. He could see through the cracks, but that's about all.

But he could still see into the basement. The basement where they had all met before the robbery was still visible, but there was no way he could enter anymore. He went as close as he could to the place where they covered the money with the concrete slabs and found that the builders had finished off the job he, Mark, and Johnny had started. Flooring was now in place over the concrete slabs. Now it was finished off with polished marble.

Steve knew for certain that the money had not been disturbed because they had placed the slabs where they were supposed to go before work on the site was suspended. Now construction had been restarted, beginning, as all structures are begun, from the ground up.

The basement floor was finished. All that was necessary were the painting and other cosmetic finishing. Yes, the money was buried under there, all right, but now they had no way to get to it. Not only because of the concrete, but there would be workmen during the day. And at night, now that the building was on its way to completion, there was bound to be security soon.

Steve looked up at a sign that bore a message revealing the name of the business that owned and would occupy the building. He blinked a couple times and stared again at the large lighted sign. Then he muttered almost soundlessly, 'I'll be a son of a bitch!'

New York Branch
The Montague Bank of Boston

CHAPTER 31

Steve and Kate

They lounged together in the warm apartment, drank from mugs of hot coffee.

'So that's it?' Kate asked.

'Pretty much.'

Kate looked at him for a moment. 'So you don't have it, and Montague doesn't have it.'

'That's about it.'

'And all the money you spent on doing it, gone?'

'Yep.'

'How much?'

'Sixty-eight thousand bucks.'

'I'm so sorry, Steve.'

'No, no, don't be. It's okay.'

Kate moved closer, put her arms around him, and snuggled her head into his neck. Then she stretched out on the sofa to get even closer. She whispered softly, 'That's too bad. I said too bad, but that doesn't seem like enough.'

'Oh, yeah, it is.'

'But you're thinking, you're thinking now, aren't you?'

'Yep.'

'How about the guys?

'That's the crazy part of it.'

'Really?'

'What did they say? I mean …'

So he told her what happened.

It was bitterly cold as they stood shivering at the building site now bank site. Steve looked them over and tried to imagine what they might be thinking. They stood staring gloomily at the place where the money was buried under the shiny marble flooring slabs. The money that was at this moment only a few feet from them but was never going to be within their reach again.

Mark, shaking his head, turned to Steve. 'Tough luck, old boy. But bloody good show.'

'Yeah,' Luke said, looking away from the bank. 'Oh, well, that's the way it goes, I guess.' Then he turned to the old man. 'Matt, I was wondering if you can still …'

'Of course, Luke.'

'Well, I guess it's like I said,' Johnny declared scratching his chin, 'it was just for laughs.'

Steve turned to the old man. 'Well, Matt, what do you say?'

Matt eyed him closely and considered his answer for a moment. When he finally spoke it was in a soft, perhaps wistful tone. 'What is there to say, my friend?' He shrugged. 'For us to say, too bad, tough luck, and as Mark said, bloody good show. Yes, all that is reasonable I suppose. But imagine, if you will, if anyone were to say, "I wish we could do it all over again," that would not be reasonable. In fact, it would be absurd, even beyond absurdity. Imagine someone foolish enough to say, "I wish we could do it all over again," utter lunacy. Whacko profundo. So being of reasonably sound mind, I will not say that.'

Steve had seen them at their worst and their best, so to speak. Now, as he watched them, he thought they looked pretty good.

Matt looked, what he actually felt—younger, fresher, stronger. Mark had an ineffable grin on his face, thinking who knows what. Luke, looking content and self-possessed, might be thinking of a story he might write one day. Not now, but one day.

Then, of course, Johnny laughed. For no reason whatsoever, Johnny laughed. And that started the others laughing.

There was no doubt that they independently had a lot of living yet to do. And no doubt that this would not be their only adventure.

After a time, they shook hands, the same way they had in the beginning. Except that this time, it was with the warmth of outright comradeship.

Then they went their separate ways.

Kate looked at him after he fished telling her what happened, perhaps trying to read what was going on in his mind. Then she burrowed her head in his arms and closed her eyes for a moment. Then she opened them again. 'So,' she said, 'the money is buried under Monty's own bank.'

'Yep, that's where it is.'

Kate sat up straight. 'You don't seem very upset.'

'You know, when you think about it, we're not that kind of people anyway, are we?'

'No we are not. We are most certainly not. I can't see either of us, or the others for that matter, strutting around with bundles of cash. You're right, Steve. That's not us.'

He nodded. 'What we are is back to where we started.'

'That's not bad. I'll take that.'

'Yeah, me too.'

They kissed, and then Kate sat back a little. 'Steve?'

'Right here.'

'You know how I want to start a small organic cosmetics company?'

'Yeah, sounds good.'

'Well, you know what? I'm going to do it! And hell, I can do that with the money I saved from my Hollywood fiasco days.'

'You can, absolutely.'

'And about the money, Steve, if you had got away with it, what were you going to do anyway? Replace an old house on the beach? You know you would never have actually done that.'

'No, that was a dream of long ago.'

'And the others, Matt and Luke, they are happy people without a lot of money.'

'And Mark. Yeah, they are. They'll be okay. Johnny too.'

They snuggled up to each other again. A contented silence descended on them for a time. Then Steve broke their shared reverie. 'I guess our inroads against the law are over.'

'Good!'

Another silence. Then, 'I'll go to see Mr Markham tomorrow.'

'And tomorrow, I'm going to give notice to my boss and start setting about starting my own organic cosmetics company. I already have a name for it—Real Face. What do you think?'

'Good name, but keep thinking.'

'Keep thinking?'

'Why not?' He scratched his chin pensively and turned to Kate, smiling. 'There's always another way.'

They were quiet for a long moment, looking at each other and smiling.

'I'll tell you something. When I was down in there, I got to thinking about an idea.'

'An idea. And?' Kate asked.

'Yes, an idea. It's a whole new thing. Yes, it involves time and in a way, motion. But I think it's a whole new concept put together with a non-traditional ...'

'You're excited about it.'

'Yeah, yeah I am.'

'Great.'

'I am excited. But you want to know something, if it flops ...'

'It won't.'

'But if it did, so what? I'd try something else.'

'Sure, like I'm going to do with the cosmetic thing. If that flops, I'll do something else.'

'Right!'

'I love you.'

'I love you too.'

Steve grinned and shook his head. But it was a positive shake. 'See, it involves an entirely new concept and—'

'Don't tell me.'

'Why not?'

'Steve, don't tell me. Tell Markham.'

'You're right! I just have to convince him that it's a viable idea. Jesus, I have to get this stuff down on paper!'

He grabbed her hands, and they danced around the room like two crazy people, whirling around to the sounds of the music in their head. Kate sprang on to the couch and then back to join him in a mad pirouette. And on and on to near exhaustion.

Suddenly, Steve stopped and looked and her.

'Wait, wait.'

'What's the matter?'

'Listen to me when you think about it.'

'Yes?'

'Well, when you think about it.'

'What? What?'

'I'm just a guy with an idea.'

Kate took him in her arms again, held him tightly. cheek to cheek, and whispered in his ear. 'Just a guy with an idea? Don't you get it, Steve? That's all it takes.'

Printed in the United States
by Baker & Taylor Publisher Services